MW01135622

SCORNFUL SCONES

A COZY CORGI MYSTERY

MILDRED ABBOTT

SCORNFUL SCONES

Mildred Abbott

for
Nancy Drew
Phryne Fisher
and
Julia South

Cover, Logo, Chapter Heading Designer: A.J. Corza - SeeingStatic.com

Main Editor: Desi Chapman

2nd Editor: Corrine Harris

Recipe and photo provided by: Rolling Pin Bakery, Denver, Co. - RollingPinBakeshop.com

Visit Mildred's Webpage: MildredAbbott.com

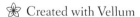 Created with Vellum

A piercing scream shattered the peaceful ambience of the bookshop. We'd closed the store ten minutes before, and I'd stolen a moment to curl up and read on the Victorian divan. At the sound, I let out a yelp and flung the book from me. Luckily it landed a few feet from the fireplace.

A clatter of claws came from the other room.

I looked over to find Watson scrambling to a standing position as quickly as his little corgi legs would allow. He glared at me as if I was the one who'd disrupted his nap in the sunshine.

Before I could make sense of a scream coming from the bookshop—it had to have come from there, as loud and clear as it had been—there was a pounding above my head followed by a squeal.

Katie?

Must be. Though I'd never heard my best friend and business partner make such a sound before.

Leaving the book on the floor of the mystery room, I hurried to the main portion of the bookshop and rushed up the stairs to the bakery two at a time, having to hike my pea-green broomstick skirt slightly to keep from tripping.

Nails still clicking on the hardwood floor, despite his slow start, Watson passed me on the staircase and entered the Cozy Corgi bakery a few strides ahead of me.

I found Katie instantly, standing behind the marble-topped bakery counter, and the mystery of the pounding was solved as she clenched her fists over her chest, performed a little jig, and let out another squeal.

Okay, apparently she wasn't in danger of dying. Although, perhaps she was possessed.

Katie caught me watching, and though a blush rose to her round cheeks, she didn't seem able to stop from giving another excited jig. With her brown curly hair bouncing around her face, she was like a little kid walking in on a surprise birthday party.

I cast a quick glance around the bakery. Atypically, the randomly arranged antique tables, rustic chairs, and overstuffed couches were unoccupied in front of the wall of windows overlooking the downtown of Estes Park. Oh, right, not that atypical, I had to remind myself; we'd closed the shop in the middle of the day.

"I'd accuse you of trying to scare away the customers, if we had any. I know we've been slammed and it's nice to have a break, but I'm pretty sure people probably heard you on the street."

"Good!" Katie squealed a third time. She literally seemed like she might be on the verge of a seizure. "I want them all to hear. And after this, we'll have a whole new definition to the word slammed. We're going to be so packed they'll be lining up all the way down the block." Another squeal.

"Katie." I crossed the bakery and took her hand over the counter. "You screamed like you just discovered zombies were real, and now you've squealed four times." I cocked an eyebrow at her but wasn't quite able to hold back the grin. "Who are you and what have you done to my best friend?"

She whipped her hand free, grasped the laptop, and spun it in my direction. "Check this out!"

I peered at the screen, at a website designed in a black-and-lavender motif with scrolling letters that read *The Sybarite* across the top. Whatever it was seemed fancy. I considered for a moment whether I was going to admit it, and then decided if Katie really was my best friend, I wouldn't be able to convince her anyway, so I just owned up to it. "Okay, I'm not really sure what I'm looking at. I don't know what a Sybarite is."

She bugged out her brown eyes as she tilted her head. "You don't know what the site is, or you don't know what the word means?"

I attempted to keep from scowling, but I was certain I failed. "Both..."

"Winifred Page! You're the most well-read woman I know. You own a bookshop. You had your own publishing company." Though there was humor in her tone, there was also genuine surprise.

"You're the one who goes on Google binges to find out random trivia. Not me. I read books to get lost in the story and a mystery. Not to throw out ten-dollar words at random." That might be true, but I did feel the sting of shame of not knowing. "Can we jump to why you're screaming like there's been another murder and skip making me feel like a fraud?"

"The site itself is my favorite food blog of all time. It's written by Maxine Maxwell. The woman has impeccable taste, on everything. But especially desserts. And this blog is a foodie's bible." She gave a combination shrug and grin that was just this side of cute. "And for future reference, *sybarite* is a person who is addicted to pleasing their senses and to luxury."

"Thank you for the vocabulary lesson." I returned my attention to the screen. "But why all the screaming? Unless this Maxine person..." I peered back up at Katie without reading any of the words, and I sucked in a breath. "She reviewed the bakery?"

Katie nodded, her smile so wide it almost looked like it hurt. "She sure did! And that was speedy, Fred. Maybe you're not quite a dictionary, but you solved that mystery almost instantaneously." She adjusted the laptop slightly so we could both see the screen and pointed halfway down the article. "I want you to read it all of course, but here's my favorite part."

I tracked to where Katie's finger was and read aloud. "It's always a delight when you find a bakery that has both ambience and delectable offerings. Tucked away on top of a charming bookshop in the middle of a picturesque mountain town, the Cozy Corgi bookshop and bakery lives up to its name. Cozy and classic—despite discovering a dog hair on my sweater when I left. I expected to find that Ms. Pizzolato's creations were a wide array of homey, comforting classics that would be found on any grandmother's table. I wasn't disappointed. Each item was well-crafted and filled with love. But beyond that, it was elevated talent, skill, and unadulterated artistry. Even the caramel tuile on top of the molasses and brown sugar brownie was pure pellucid perfection. I was transported to heaven." The words stopped, so I scrolled up to reveal more of the article, and discovered pictures of the brownie in question, shots of the entire bakery, a wide encompassing image of the bookshop, as well as the view of the outside of the Cozy Corgi from the street. "Wow! This is amazing."

Katie squealed again, and I couldn't blame her. "Pure pellucid perfection. That's what she said my caramel tuile is. Pure pellucid perfection. She's right, of course, but still." She paused in her celebration to offer a cocked eyebrow of her own. "Just so you know, Fred, pellucid means that the caramel is—"

"Oh, shut up!" I swiped at her playfully while laughing. "It means she could see through the tuile. I got it, I'm not a complete heathen."

Katie chuckled, glanced back at the computer screen, and sucked in a breath like she discovered it all over again. "We are on the Sybarite! Can you believe it?" As if her happiness was threatening to cause her to combust, Katie let out another yelp and then danced another jig.

Watson let out a grumpy growl and took several steps back from the counter.

Katie leaned over and scrunched her nose at him. "Oh, sorry, buddy. Here, let me make it up to you." She quickly retrieved one of his favorite all-natural dog bone treats from a hidden compartment behind the counter and tossed it to him.

Watson was my heart and my hero, but an athlete, he was not. Though he attempted to catch it, the treat bounced off his nose and went careening over the floor. Once again, little corgi feet struggled for traction on the hardwood as he ran in place for a second and then darted after it. Once he'd captured the treat, he lifted his head regally and pranced in a dignified manner to a spot under one of the far tables to eat in peace.

I loved that little freak.

After a second, I turned back to Katie and the computer. "This really is amazing. And well-deserved. I've never met anyone who bakes as well as you."

"Thanks, Fred. That means the world." She blushed again, clearly pleased. "But this really is huge, and I'm honored, it was so unexpected. I know we're not needing more crowds—we're barely getting by the way it is—but it could draw people who follow her blog to visit the shop. People travel all over the country at the suggestions of this woman. They'll plan entire trips to Estes Park just for our bakery." Her smile faltered. "Talk about pressure."

I was feeling that myself, and the review hadn't really even been about the bookshop portion. I couldn't imagine what Katie was feeling. "Don't think about it. You just bake like you always do, and everyone will love it. Don't stress yourself out." That was easier said than done, and I knew it. I could also see that the thought was starting to steal some of Katie's joy, which squealing or not, I didn't want to see diminished. "Did you know that Maxine Maxwell had come in? You didn't mention it."

"No." The distraction worked instantly, some of the wonder returning to Katie's expression. "You know, I hadn't even thought of that. But thank goodness I didn't know. I would've been a complete wreck waiting on her, and then an absolute mess wondering what she'd thought and if she was going to post about it." She clutched at her chest. "Holy moly, what if she hadn't liked it. I could've opened up to my favorite blog and seen her ripping apart my bakery."

"But she didn't rip it apart." I reached for Katie's hand again. "Obviously the woman has taste, because she didn't do that. She saw your baking for what it is. Your pure pellucid perfection. Exactly what anyone addicted to... what was it... the finer things in life has come to expect?"

"To the pleasure of the senses and luxury, actually." She winked. "I'll quiz you later."

"You're enjoying this a little too much." I chuckled and released her hand with a final squeeze. "So happy for the review, Katie. It really is wonderful."

"Yeah. It really is." Katie sighed contentedly, then sucked in a breath as she straightened. "Oh no. I hadn't even thought. We're going to Black Bear Roaster in just a few minutes. What if Carla has seen this? She'll be livid."

Now that was a thought. Things were tense enough between Carla and the two of us; the review of Katie's baking wasn't going to help anything. "I'm sure she hasn't seen it. She's too busy setting up for the celebration. They're doing it open-house style, people have been coming in and out all day I'm sure. I doubt she's had a second to look. Besides, who knows if she even reads that blog. It's not like she makes her own items at the coffee shop."

"Oh, she reads it. And she wants to be on it. Don't kid yourself." She considered for a second and nodded. "But I bet you're right. No way she's had time to see it. I've glanced out the windows every once in a while. They're keeping pretty busy down there."

We'd already had this discussion several times over the past week, but I decided to give it one more shot. "We could stay here, just to be on the safe side. We can even stay closed for the hour like we planned. You can get some more baking done, I can get some more reading accomplished. Watson can nap. Just avoid it altogether."

Katie pointed her finger at me, suddenly serious. "Don't try to get out of this, Fred. This is a show of goodwill. Besides, the invitation stated that dogs were welcome. Clearly that was directed at you, since you helped clear her name not that long ago. We can't skip it. Maybe this will be the thing that puts us on equal footing again. If we were ever there to begin with."

I narrowed my eyes at her. "You just want to go so you can wear your new T-shirt."

She didn't even pretend to deny it as she pulled out the hem of her T-shirt so she could get a better view at the embossed image of two large cups of coffee sitting at a tea party, dining on scones. "Well, I did have Joe make it special. It would be a shame to waste it."

"Yeah, a real shame. The whole world needs to see that." Katie and I never agreed on fashion. Not that I cared either way, but it was fun to tease her about it. "Still, I know you, Katie. You're not fooling me. You picked scones because they're the worst things there."

"I'd say that's subjective." That accusation she *did* attempt to deny, though she didn't quite pull it off. "Who can really say what's the best or the worst anywhere." Her smile returned, and then she pointed to the computer. "Although, I suppose Maxine Maxwell might have a thought or two about what's the best."

"I'm never going to hear the end of this, am I?"

She shook her head. "Nope."

Black Bear Roaster was packed. So much so that it reminded me of how Katie's bakery had been recently. Having a celebration for introducing the new line of espresso in honor of her son, who was born two months before, was rather genius on Carla's part. And I didn't begrudge her for thinking of it. The coffee shop was Carla's livelihood, her passion, and though the bakery on top of my little bookshop had been Katie's dream, not mine, I couldn't help but feel responsible for Carla losing business. Although... her personality and cardboardesque food might have had something to do with it.

Watson had been prancing on our way to the front door—he didn't have a problem with the cardboard flavor of Carla's offerings—but he halted as we walked inside and found the crowd. He let out a low mixture of a whine and growl as he glared at the countless feet between him and the case of pastries.

Katie chuckled and bent down to scratch his head. "You and your mama are quite a bit alike sometimes."

"What? I'm not growling."

She grinned at me and stood once more. "You sure about that?"

I gave her a glare, doing my best to match Watson's.

Right on cue, Carla emerged from under a blue banner strung over the rear portion of the store reading *Introducing Maverick Espresso*. On the left side was a picture of a fuzzy teddy bear, and on the right, a steaming cup of coffee. As Carla had named her son Maverick Espresso Beaker, I wasn't sure whether the sign was celebrating the newborn or the espresso. Maybe this had been a new launch and a baby welcoming combined. I hadn't even thought to bring a baby present.

Carla hurried over to us, swiping her blonde bangs over her forehead. "You made it. I'm so glad." She pulled me into a hug, patted my back, did the same to Katie, and then lowered herself to rub Watson behind the ears.

He stiffened, but allowed himself to be touched.

Katie and I exchanged glances. This was a new version of Carla Beaker I'd never met before. Maybe motherhood really did change a person.

I barely had time to figure out what to say before she stood back up.

"Of course we're here. We wouldn't have missed it." I kept my gaze firmly away from Katie, lest I see the smirk I was certain was plastered on her face. "We're so excited about your new espresso. Both of them."

There was a silent heartbeat.

"Both the baby and the coffee," Katie clarified.

Carla rolled her eyes. "Oh, of course. Sorry. I've only heard that fifty thousand times today. Should have caught on." Ah, there she was. Good. All felt right in the world once more. But no sooner had the real Carla Beaker flashed behind her eyes than the

Stepford version emerged once more. "Please make yourself at home. I'm afraid I must play hostess, and I'm sorry that Maverick isn't here. Jonathan just took him home for naptime. But come back by later this afternoon; hopefully, he'll be here again."

She started to walk away, then turned back, giving the gesture over her shoulder toward the counter. "I should let you know, my grandfather, Harold, is helping out since Maverick's birth." I followed her motion and saw an old, tired-looking man staring at the case of pastries with a lost expression. On either side of him stood the two teenage baristas, a boy and girl. "Please be patient with him. He's excited to have more time out of the nursing home, but I think it's all a little overwhelming." Her nostrils flared, little bits of the original Carla showing through as she cast a side-eye at Katie. "It's hard to get featured in a premier blog when my life is nothing but diapers, teenagers with acne, and the geriatric." Without any other transition, Carla turned and stopped by the closest table, where Paulie Mertz, the owner of the pet shop, was seated.

He noticed us and gave an overly enthusiastic wave.

I waved back but stepped toward the counter instead. The strange little man had grown on me, but

I didn't feel up to dealing with him and Carla at the same time.

"Told you that she'd read the blog." Katie followed Watson and me. "But still, that was bizarre. It was the nicest I've ever seen that woman. But it also felt like she was one breath away from leaning over and ripping out my throat with her teeth."

I snorted out a laugh. "Good grief, Katie. Gruesome much?"

She shrugged, unconcerned. "And she didn't even comment on my T-shirt. I mean, really? Could it be more perfect?"

"That is a pretty great T-shirt, Katie." The male version of the teenage barista flashed Katie a smile though his hands never stopped moving on the espresso machine, eliciting puffs of steam and foam as if he was a conductor. "But it would've been better if that unicorn hippo character you wear so much was present."

"Dang it!" Katie shook her fist toward the barista. "Nick, I didn't even think about it. That would've been brilliant. I'm coming to you from now on whenever I come up with a new design."

I marveled at the two of them. Since moving to Estes Park the previous winter, I'd been in Black Bear Roaster countless times, at least before I had

Katie making heaven above my head. I'd seen both of the teenage baristas countless times. Not once had I seen either of them ever appear anything other than sullen. And I most definitely never learned their names. I had quite literally only seen the boy and thought *teenage barista*. Apparently, his name was Nick. And also apparently, I was a horrible person. He and the girl had offered me the elixir of life in the form of a dirty chai how many times? And I'd never bothered to learn their names.

As if to rub it in, the teenage barista—er... Nick—offered a smile-like grimace at me. "I suppose you want your normal dirty chai, Ms. Page?" Though not unfriendly, the chipper quality he'd used with Katie vanished, and he seemed sullen once more, and rather nervous.

"Yes. That would be wonderful. Thank you, Nick."

His dark eyes flashed at me in surprise, then refocused on his task.

I was a good tipper, but I'd have to leave an extra-large one today in way of apology.

As Nick fixed Katie's and my drinks, Carla's grandfather—I had to consider for a moment to recall his name—Harold, offered a smile from behind the case of pastries. His gleaming white dentures seemed a little too large for his face but provided him a rather affable quality. "Well, hey there, pretty ladies and hairy pooch. Any delicacies I can offer you?"

"I'd love your blueberry streusel muffin, please." Katie smiled at him in her good-natured way, but over the long process of Harold separating one pastry bag from another and struggling to get it open and then the small war of sliding the muffin inside, her smile grew strained.

It was hard to watch. The man was clearly out of his comfort zone. His hands never ceased trembling as he worked.

By the time he looked at me, I almost felt guilty for ordering something. "I think I'll do your apple cinnamon scone, please."

He beamed, friendly once more, though a trail of sweat made its way down his temple. "Would you like the apple butter on top that comes with it?"

I would, but I couldn't fathom putting him through that process. "No, but thank you." I patted my stomach. "Gotta watch the figure."

Katie cast me a quizzical glance. Those four words were not in our vocabulary.

Still shaking, Harold repeated the process, and when he slid a pumpkin scone into the bag, I didn't correct him. It wasn't like it mattered; Watson would end up eating over half of it anyway.

After a few more minutes, Katie and I had our drinks and pastries, we'd paid, and managed to find a recently vacated two-top over in the corner.

Katie scowled as she whispered, "I don't know if it's nice that Carla gave her grandfather a job here, or if it's nice that her grandfather is helping her out? The whole thing seemed rather painful."

"No kidding." I pointed at her, only partially teasing. "You are *not* allowed to offer him a job to try to rescue him. We can't steal any more of Carla's employees. If we do, she'll take out a hit on us—I have no doubt."

Katie chuckled. "I won't. Although you've got to admit; that would be kind of hilarious. Having Carla's grandfather come over and work for me in the bakery."

"You're a sick woman, Katie. And once more I'm reminded why we get along so well." I tore off a bit of my scone. After one bite, it did what Carla's scones always did and soaked up every bit of moisture so my mouth felt like the Sahara. I tore off another bite and passed it covertly to Watson under the table.

He shivered in pleasure.

"So—" I leaned across the table, closer to Katie,

"—how long do you think we have to stay here to not be rude?"

"I'd say about fifteen minutes will be good."

"Fifteen minutes? That's a little exorbitant, don't you think?"

Katie patted my hand. "By that time, you'll be able to get a second dirty chai."

She had a point.

The longer we sat there, the more pleasant it became. It was fun watching the endless stream of townspeople pass by. And truly amazing how much gossip a person could catch up on just by sitting still and listening.

Before getting my second drink, I left Watson with Katie and went to the restroom. It was occupied, but there wasn't a line, so I waited in the narrow hall toward the back.

"He's nothing more than an embarrassment, Carla. This has to end." The man's voice was angry and low, and it took me a second to realize it was coming from the door that was open a crack at the end of the hall.

"He's my grandfather, Eustace. And this is *my* coffee shop." Carla's voice drifted to me—though it too was quiet, it was sharp and somewhat vicious. "I know it's a foreign concept to you, but you don't rule the entire world."

"You wouldn't have this coffee shop if it weren't for my son and our money."

Not bothering to try talking myself out of my natural impulse—the expression "curiosity killed the cat" was a warning I'd abandoned months ago—I eased my way down the hall and managed to look through the open doorway. Though I couldn't see Carla, I saw Eustace Beaker, her father-in-law. I'd never had any real interaction with the man other than him and his wife coming into the store on opening night, but he served on the town council with my uncle, Percival, and I'd heard plenty of stories.

"Jonathan helped me get Black Bear Roaster up and running, but it pays the bills every month, thank you very much. We're not a drain on you or your fortune." Carla might not be my favorite person in the world, but I couldn't help admiring the way she stood up to her father-in-law as well as the conviction in her voice.

"You might not be a drain, but you're an embarrassment. This whole coffee shop is. It was bad enough you have the Indian kid working for you when he can't even graduate high school on time; now you bring in your decrepit grandfather?" Eustace sneered.

The man was repulsive. And from the looks of him, though moneyed and well put together, I figured he wasn't that much younger than Carla's grandfather.

And the Indian kid? Seriously?

"Nick is a good kid and leave my grandfather out of this. He's helping me out. It does him good. He needs a break from the nursing home from time to time." While Carla kept speaking, Eustace must've felt my stare and glanced over at me.

His eyes narrowed, and I gave a little flinch at being caught.

Just then, there was a click as the door to the women's restroom opened and Myrtle Bantam emerged. Thankfully she didn't notice me or call out my name. As she walked back into the coffee shop, I slipped into the bathroom as quickly as I could and locked the door.

My time in the bathroom was so excessive I nearly started counting the tiles on the floor. Why I'd ducked into the lavatory instead of booking it for the front door, I didn't know. Talk about stupid. There wasn't even a tiny window to try to crawl out of. Probably for the best. With my luck I knew exactly how that would end. Either with me getting stuck halfway through or accidentally leaving my skirt behind. What a great start to the tourist season that would be—the local bookshop owner caught in the streets in nothing but her long red hair, silver corgi earrings, peasant blouse, and cowboy boots.

Although... if Carla and her father-in-law were standing outside the bathroom door waiting for me, doing a partial streak through the downtown didn't sound half bad by comparison.

Finally, there was a knock at the door and the handle jiggled.

"Sorry, one second!" I glanced at the back wall. No, still no window. What if it was Carla and Eustace knocking?

Well, what of it? *He* should be ashamed of himself, not me. I reached for the door handle, then paused, thinking I needed to keep some semblance of my pride. Though I hadn't used either, I went over, flushed the toilet and then washed and dried my hands, just in case they were listening.

When I finally opened the door, it was the other teenage barista. Her blue eyes were wide in panicked frustration, like she'd been waiting awhile at a very inopportune time.

"Sorry. The chai wasn't sitting right." The words were out of my mouth before I could think about them. So much for my pride.

The girl ducked past me with a grossed-out shudder.

I blocked the door with my hand before it closed, as another thought hit me. "I've been coming here for months, granted not as much as I used to, but still. I've never asked your name." *Really? This is what I was doing right then?*

She gaped at me like I was insane. At least she was a good judge of character. "Um... Tiffany?"

She didn't sound overly sure of that, but maybe she was a little terrified of me.

"Well, it's nice to meet you, Tiffany. Sorry I never asked before."

She only stared at my hands still holding the door ajar.

"Oh, sorry!" I pulled my hand away, letting the door close. There was an instant click of the lock. I glanced back toward the stockroom where Carla and Eustace had been. I didn't hear anything. At least they weren't waiting.

If I hadn't been ready to head for the hills before, I most definitely was after my interaction with Tiffany. Poor thing. Keeping my gaze firmly two paces ahead of my feet, I hurried back into the main portion of the coffee shop and darted toward the table where I'd left Katie. I was going to grab Watson's leash and make a run for it.

But oh, the plans of mice and men...

Paulie and his friends had joined Katie at the table. And he was currently on his knees lavishing affection on a very unappreciative Watson. Noticing me, he grinned but didn't stop his stroking of Watson's sides. "I haven't seen your little man in forever. You haven't come in for dog food lately."

"Well, he's a little finicky. He's stopped eating any sort of dog food. Now I have to cook for him constantly." It was true enough. And after buying two exorbitantly priced bags of dog food that ended up going to the squirrels and chipmunks, it was time for Paulie to know the truth.

Katie peered over her shoulder at me in concern. "You were gone a long time. Are you okay?"

I nearly made another comment like I had with Tiffany, but then I glanced at Paulie's friend, an older African American woman who could have just stepped off the pages of *Vogue*. For once, my brain caught up with my mouth. "Oh yes, just fine. Thank you."

Before I could figure out an appropriate excuse to get Katie and me to leave, Paulie was standing and making introductions. "I don't know if you guys have met. Fred, this is Athena Rose. She writes the obituaries for the paper."

"I've been in your charming bookstore a couple of times, although I don't think we've officially been introduced." She held out a french-tipped hand. "And I have to thank you. My role at the paper is staying much busier since you moved to town." Her eyes twinkled.

I shook her hand, considering her words, then realized the implication since she wrote obituaries. "Well, I don't know if I can take credit for that. I might've discovered a few dead bodies, but I'm hardly responsible for them."

She gave a prim shrug. "Maybe so, but you most definitely make it more interesting."

"Athena has a little teacup poodle named Pearl that my boys love to play with." Paulie pulled the attention back to himself and finally stopped petting Watson and took his seat as he motioned toward the empty one between him and Katie. It seemed I'd been gone so long our tiny table for two had become an even tinier table for four.

Athena held up her purse from her lap, and a tiny fluffy white head smiled at me.

"Oh my goodness. That's the most adorable thing I've ever seen. She hardly looks real." I couldn't imagine the tiny dog surviving a solitary minute with Paulie's two crazy corgis. I turned back to him. "How are Flotsam and Jetsam? You didn't bring them? The invitation said dogs are welcome."

He shook his head. "No, not my boys. They're banned from here for life. The last time I brought them in, Flotsam wouldn't quit humping Carla's leg, and while I was trying to get him to stop, Jetsam ran back into the storeroom and ate through an entire shipment of coffeecake."

That sounded about right, but at the mention of the storeroom, I glanced back the way I had come. Carla was behind the counter, helping her grandfather with something. Nick was still manning the espresso machine, and Tiffany apparently was taking her own sweet time in the bathroom as well. For a moment, I didn't see Eustace, which made me hope he'd left.

But then I found him, standing across the shop next to an overdressed woman I assumed was his wife, holding a plate with an untouched scone as he glared. And that glare flicked back and forth between Carla and me. I jolted when his dark blue eyes met mine. Clearly, I couldn't play it off that I hadn't overheard them.

I whipped back around, hoping he wouldn't come over.

Once more, Katie was studying me. "Are you sure you're okay? You seem a little off."

"Yeah, I'm fine. We should probably get back to the Cozy Corgi soon, don't you think?" I tried to infuse my voice with an ease I didn't feel. "Surely we've been here more than fifteen minutes?"

Before Katie could respond, Athena's sharp gaze

tracked from Eustace to me. "It appears Mr. Beaker isn't your biggest fan."

She was blunt; I had to give her that. "Well... we haven't really interacted that much. He probably just doesn't like that his daughter-in-law's competition is here."

Before I could stop her, Katie craned around like a busybody in church.

I swatted at her. "Katie. Turn back around."

She did, but didn't seemed overly concerned about being caught staring. "Oh, he's a nightmare. He and his wife. They would come in when I worked here every once in a while and raise absolute havoc. Carla wasn't the easiest boss, but she was nothing compared to those two."

Despite the background noise of the crowded coffee shop being enough to counter Katie's voice, I shushed her.

Athena waved me off. "Oh, don't bother. It's no secret. Anyone who's met the man knows he's nothing more than a loathsome, imperious tyrant."

Blunt indeed.

I stared at her for a second, then couldn't suppress a grin. "You might just be my new favorite person."

"Well, then, apparently you have exquisite taste." She winked, and I realized she was wearing false eyelashes. Athena Rose was more glamorous sitting in the middle of a coffee shop with her teacup poodle in a purse than I'd been on my wedding day to my ex-husband. Women like her were always a marvel to me.

Paulie lowered his voice, showing more reserve than what I'd typically observed from him. "He is awful. Remember I told you some of the town council had given me a hard time when I moved to town? He was one of the ringleaders in that. If it wasn't for your uncle speaking up for me, I doubt I'd own the pet shop."

It seemed my initial reaction to the man had been correct. Not that it was any real surprise, given how he'd treated Carla and spoken of Harold and Nick, but still.

Paulie, Athena, and Katie continued to gossip about Eustace and his wife, Ethel. It seemed they felt they were town royalty. I came in and out of the conversation, as I allowed my attention to wander while I surveyed the busy coffee shop. It was only the middle of May and already the tourist season was picking up, just like I'd been promised. It would be in full force in a few weeks when school was out. Hopefully, with the new rush of people, things would even out between Carla's coffee shop and Katie's bakery. I knew there would naturally be some competition, but it would be wonderful if it was less acute.

Even so, it was clear Katie had made the right choice in interviewing possible helpers later that afternoon. It'd been a couple of months since her other assistant baker had been murdered. Though it felt disrespectful to think of replacing Sammy, we couldn't keep going like we were. Still, watching Carla made me question if it was really all that much help doing interviews.

She was flitting back and forth between her three employees. One second growling something in irritation at Tiffany, then rolling her eyes at Nick, only to seem close to frustrated tears at something her grandfather did. And through it all, she was doing her best to smile and be welcoming to all the friends and customers crowding her shop.

I'd have to make sure to find the right person to help me at the bookshop, or it would simply cause more work.

Carla truly did seem frazzled and overwhelmed, alternating between a frantic smile and her cheeks flushing in what appeared to be temper. I'd noticed that temper many times before, but it seemed even closer to the surface than usual. Granted, given the exchange with her father-in-law, I couldn't blame her. Especially with him still standing there scowling in the middle of it all.

Even as I watched, he left his wife's side from their position of judgment to join Carla behind the counter, where he began to quietly rail at something Nick had done, all the while holding his plated scone.

For his part, the teenager simply ducked his eyes and nodded, clearly humiliated, but not like he was about to talk back. It was almost impressive, the kid had more restraint than me.

Carla said something to Eustace that I couldn't hear, but she looked furious as she stomped off toward the backroom again.

Her grandfather started to follow her, concern etched over his old face, but at a snarl from Eustace, he stayed where he was.

For his part, Eustace picked up his scone, took a bite, and leaned against the back counter to observe. His judgmental stare traveled over the three employees, then met mine. He took another bite and kept staring.

I started to turn away like I had the first two times, then felt like it was almost a dare. As if he was testing me somehow. I lifted my chin and stared back. I'd allowed myself to be bullied by my ex-husband from time to time, and I promised I'd never let anyone do that to me again. And though no words were tossed in my direction, his intention was clear.

He cocked an eyebrow, almost seemed surprised, but only took another bite of the scone.

It was a strange sensation, this moment linking Eustace and me, both of us situated across the coffee shop from each other with several people between. This challenge with a man I hadn't interacted with yet had been caught eavesdropping on as he berated his daughter-in-law.

Katie was saying something to me, but I didn't respond, didn't even catch her words. Maybe it was ridiculous or silly, although it didn't feel like it, but I was not going to lose the battle of wills with Mr. Beaker, even if I had to sit there staring at him until closing.

He took another bite of the scone. It looked like the white chocolate cranberry with the crusting of powdered sugar over the top.

His eyes narrowed slightly, and then Eustace lost the staring match.

He choked, let out a cough, and blinked.

Okay, maybe he lost the staring match by default, but still.

He choked again, beat on his chest a couple of times, and then took off toward the hallway leading to the lavatory and storeroom.

Well, choked or not, he'd remember that I hadn't blinked. I sat back, oddly satisfied.

"What in the green blazes was that?" Katie stared at me.

I started to answer, then paused. "You know... I'm not exactly sure. But whatever it was, I won." I couldn't keep from grinning.

"I guess that's all that matters. Turns out, I'm not the only competitive one." She grinned as she patted my hand. "Ready to go? I heard a rumor that you sell books and I make pastries. I suppose we should act like it."

"Yes. Let's." I glanced at her companions. "It was great to see you again, Paulie. And a pleasure to meet you, Athena."

"Was good to see you too, Fred. How about a playdate for the pups soon?"

Before I could figure out an excuse, Athena rescued me. "Trust me, sweetie, the pleasure was all mine. You just keep making the obituaries more interesting for me, and we'll be in good shape." She turned to Paulie. "Darling, do you think you can fetch me a fresh Earl Grey?"

"Of course." Paulie offered a smile to Katie and me and didn't wait to confirm the playdate.

A cut of guilt sliced through me; it was probably obvious I'd been avoiding answering. In my defense, Watson really truly detested Flotsam and Jetsam.

Katie and I had just stood, and I was gathering up Watson's leash from under the table, when a scream cut through the coffee shop.

The second scream of the day didn't startle me like the first, and somehow I recognized the voice, although I suppose how wasn't a mystery, considering I'd heard Carla's raised tone more than once.

The entire coffee shop froze in place, every voice stilled. After the scene I'd just witnessed between Carla and her father-in-law, I had a vision of him slapping her or something. Dropping the leash, I rushed from our table toward the hallway that led to the backroom, Watson on my heels. Not only was I going to show Eustace Beaker that I wasn't going to be beaten down in a staring contest, but that no matter the strain in his daughter-in-law's and my relationship, I wasn't going to let him trounce all over her when I was present.

As I rounded the hallway, such thoughts fled as I found Eustace sprawled on the floor in front of the bathroom door, Carla standing over him. Her hand was over her mouth, and she looked up at me, her eyes wide once more. "He's dead. I think he's dead."

Watson tromping down the steps alerted me that he and Leo were coming from the bakery. Despite park ranger Leo Lopez's muscular frame, he could move as silently as a ghost through the forest or a bookshop. My furry, possibly overly fluffy, little man... not so much.

I watched them approach from my spot reading by the fire. The interruption was welcome. It wasn't like I'd been able to concentrate on the book anyway —too many thoughts rolling around in my head.

Leo didn't have to search to find me. Where else would I be other than tucked away in my favorite spot of the store? He motioned to the other end of the antique sofa, as Watson pranced adoringly at his feet. "Do you mind if I join you?"

I'd abandoned my boots at the counter half an hour before, so I moved my socked feet over, making room. "Katie kick you out?"

He nodded with a grin. "I can't tell if she's more nervous or more guilty. Either way, I guarantee you she's more of a mess than the people she's going to interview shortly. Between feeling like she's betraying Sammy and now wondering about continuing with the scheduled interviews on the same day as another death, she's overthinking everything."

She must be struggling more than I'd realized if she'd shoved Leo aside. "Maybe I should go talk to her again."

"No." Leo reached out a hand and touched my wrist, halting me. "I think she just needs to work through it on her own for a little bit. She still wants you there during the interviews." He withdrew his hand almost instantly and lowered it to stroke Watson who sat by Leo's feet. He refocused on the fire. "It's the middle of May, Fred. I know it's not beach weather, but surely you're not cold."

"I know, but it's just so beautiful and relaxing. Granted, I'm not in a rush for the snow to come back, but there really is nothing like reading by a fire." That was the other reason I'd taken off my boots. The hair at the back of my neck was damp with sweat. I was warm enough that the fire was the furthest thing from relaxing. More like stifling, but I was stubborn. Hopefully I'd let that go by the time July hit.

With his free hand, Leo unfastened the second button of his shirt and fanned the fabric to cool himself off while unintentionally revealing a flash of honey-brown skin.

I averted my eyes. I wasn't sure what was going on between him and Katie. The three of us had most definitely become the Three Amigos of Estes Park over the past several months, and half the time I was certain that was all that was happening with him and Katie, but then at others, it seemed like more. And even if I'd thought Leo was interested in me at the beginning, I wasn't going to stand in my friend's way. Not that there was any reason to. Leo and I were just friends. And if I wore the dangling silver earrings in the shape of corgis that Leo had given me nearly every day, it was just because I liked them, not because of any secret intentions.

"Winifred Page discovers another dead body, huh?" He cast a sidelong glance my way.

I latched on to the topic. "I don't think I can claim that distinction this time around. Carla was the one who screamed. She was there before me."

"Maybe so, but still. You do have a certain knack." A playful grin cut his face.

"Everyone keeps saying that. Even the obituary writer I met today, Athena, mentioned that I helped make her job a lot more fun lately." I bugged my eyes out at him in a teasing manner. "I'm not going around killing people, if you recall."

"I don't think anyone's going to accuse you of killing Eustace Beaker, considering he choked to death in the middle of the coffee shop."

"Well..." And hence the reason I hadn't been able to focus on my book. "He wasn't exactly in the middle of the coffee shop. True, I did notice him choking, but no one actually saw him die. Even Carla says she walked out of the back room and found him dead in the hallway."

Forgetting Watson for the moment, Leo twisted, angling more fully toward me. "I know that sound in your voice, Fred. You think he was murdered."

I shook my head. "I didn't say that."

He narrowed his eyes, his grin returning slightly. "You didn't have to."

Watson propped his forepaws on the edge of the sofa and nudged Leo's hand roughly with his nose while giving a scolding chuff. While there were moments I wasn't sure what feelings existed between Leo and me, and Leo and Katie, there was no doubt Watson was head over heels in love with the handsome park ranger. Although I doubted his looks had anything to do with it. For his part, Leo seemed just as enamored of Watson.

"Sorry, buddy. I forgot my job, didn't I?" He made up for his error by lavishing attention on Watson with both hands, but refocused on me. "What do you think happened? Poison?"

I flinched, surprised that Leo had reached that conclusion so quickly. "Maybe the thought crossed my mind."

"That would be one fast-acting poison, wouldn't it?"

I shrugged. "I'm not an expert on poisons, but you're probably right."

"I'm not doubting your intelligence or ability, Fred." He sounded hesitant, like he was afraid I'd be offended. "And I know there's been a lot of murders in town since you've moved here, but sometimes people die on their own. Accidents happen."

And that had been the other refrain floating through my mind in between the possibilities of Eustace Beaker being murdered. "I know. But... the man was awful. Granted, I was only around him for a matter of minutes today, but he was awful. And from what I could see and what I heard from other people, it sounds like that was a pretty common state of being for him." With someone else, I might've felt the need to apologize for speaking ill of the dead so quickly after their departure. But this wasn't Leo's and my first rodeo.

"As opposed to the song, not only the good die young."

"He was hardly young." I chuckled, then sobered. "Goodness, listen to us. Talking about a man's death as lightly as if we're discussing the possibility of a whodunit in a movie. A man just died. Someone's husband, someone's father. Little Maverick's grandfather."

Leo opened his mouth, then paused as he seemed to consider. After a couple of seconds, he nodded. "Maybe so, but we're not exactly strangers to death, and we don't have any connection to Eustace. Plus, it seems like most of the ones who did weren't better for it. We don't have to throw a party that he's gone, but I don't think we have to pretend to grieve either."

I agreed, but it was something I needed to stay aware of.

The beat of Katie's pacing footsteps in the bakery sounded over the soft piped-in music. We both glanced up.

"She's going to drive herself crazy."

Leo nodded, but didn't change the topic. "What did Branson say?"

The question threw me. "What do you mean?"

Leo looked confused. "Once you saw him at Carla's when Eustace died. What did he say about your theory?"

"Oh!" I shook my head. "He wasn't there. He's out of town for a couple of days. Officer Green was the one who came to the scene."

"I take it you didn't tell her your suspicions?"

"No. Not hardly." Susan Green and I had disliked each other from the moment we met. Actually, she disliked me first, but I was quick to follow suit. Over the past few months, there were moments where I thought we might form a friendship, or something similar. But it often felt like one step forward, two steps back.

Leo licked his lips and focused on Watson's hero-worship-filled eyes. "Sergeant Wexler did a great job officiating the Duck Race Festival last week. The two of you seem to be getting on pretty well."

Every May, Estes Park had a fundraiser where people would buy rubber ducks with a raffle number on the bottom. The city dumped thousands of them in the river, and whichever ones made it to the finish line the fastest were the prizewinners. The event raised massive amounts of money for charity. It had been Branson's turn to be the announcer.

I studied Leo before responding. He kept his gaze firmly fixed to Watson. Maybe I was reading into it too much. Although, it was odd that he referred to Branson so formally. But he'd been right, Branson and I had had our ups and downs, but we'd been in a smooth spot lately. "We're going to dinner when he gets back in town."

There was no reaction from Leo. None at all.

Was that, in and of itself, a reaction? I couldn't tell.

I also wasn't entirely sure why I had told Leo about our upcoming date. Was I trying to get a reaction? Leo and I were just friends, after all. Friends told each other these things. I'd told Katie. And I'd studied her for a reaction as well. Seeing if there might be disapproval or excitement. Maybe this was the same thing.

Though it felt different.

"Dinner. Dinner is... delicious." Leo finally spoke and cleared his throat. When he looked over at me, his tone was back to normal and there was no hint of anything in his eyes. "Well, I suppose that's depending on where you go."

Before I could figure out how to respond, the

front door handle of the Cozy Corgi jiggled, followed by a sharp knock.

I took the excuse and stood quickly. "I guess someone must be here early for the interview. I'll go grab my boots if you want to let Katie know." Not waiting for a response, I left the mystery room and headed toward the main counter to retrieve my boots. Leaving Leo, Watson followed at my feet. As I entered the main portion of the bookshop, I noticed the face staring in from the front door.

I paused, dread washing over me at the sight of Officer Susan Green with her hand pressed above her eyes, attempting to peer in.

No, not dread. I wasn't sure what. But something.

Maybe I was right about my Eustace Beaker theory after all.

As I slid on my boots, I called out over my shoulder, "Never mind, it's just Susan."

"Susan?" Leo's voice rose an octave behind me. "Huh, maybe you're onto something after all, Winifred."

Great minds thought alike.

Once again in both of my boots and Watson prancing beside me, I unlocked the front door and held it open for Officer Green.

Susan scowled as she stepped in.

As soon as he realized who it was, Watson growled softly.

She glared down at him. "Yeah, well, I don't really like you either, furball." Susan focused on me, but then her gaze flitted over my shoulder, her pale blue eyes widening. "Oh. Interesting. While the thought of your love life quite literally turns my stomach, Ms. Page, should I let my superior know he has competition while he's away?"

I wasn't sure if my name or the word superior was spoken with more disdain. And it looked like this interaction was going to be two steps back. Possibly three or four. "Leo and I are friends. Anything Sergeant Wexler and I are, or are not, isn't your concern, *Officer* Green."

She bristled at my far from subtle dig at her station.

"You know, I think Katie's probably needing..." Leo's voice faltered, then he let out a small chuckle. "I'll be upstairs. You ladies have fun."

I hated that Leo had seen me in that moment, but not nearly as much as I hated that I still allowed myself to have moments like this with Susan Green. My temper got the best of me at times. But my inter-actions with Susan were often something different.

One that I truly despised. I'd come to realize she felt the same. Whatever it was we did to each other, neither of us liked. But it also seemed we weren't quite able to manage our reactions either.

I bent down and patted Watson on the head, though he didn't quit growling. "Go with Leo. I'll be fine."

Watson glanced up at me, probably disconcerted at the mention of Leo's name while having his own strong reaction to Susan.

"Go on." I motioned back toward the steps, lilting my voice. "Leo and Katie. They have a snack for you."

Susan forgotten, Watson gave a little bunny hop of his front paws, his fox ears somehow managing to point even more skyward.

"Yep! Treat!" Another motion up the steps. "Go get a treat."

And he was off. Running so fast his back legs stumbled on the first step, but then they got a hold, and he disappeared.

I used the distraction to remind myself that I was a civilized adult woman capable of having self-control and not being a snarky seventh grader. I even managed a smile I didn't think was overly saccharine. "What can I do for you, Susan?"

"Officer Green, remember?"

I took a slow breath and turned around, giving myself another moment, then headed back toward the mystery room. "Follow me, Officer Green. We can have a seat while we chat."

To my surprise, she didn't argue, and within a few moments we were both seated at either end of the sofa. Though similar to how Leo and I had sat only minutes before, it felt like the couch had gained an extra few yards.

"Good grief, it's as hot as an oven in here." Susan wiggled, shifting the holstered gun on her hips slightly. "And this fancy thing sure isn't comfortable, is it?" Her gaze lifted to the antique lamp with the purple fabric and fringed shade. "Kinda prissy too."

She was in a mood. Most definitely. I decided to cut through it. I didn't have the energy, I never felt good about myself afterward, and Katie and I had interviews arriving any second. "I take it you're here because of Eustace Beaker?"

She stopped studying the lampshade to stare at me in suspicion. "Interesting that you'd assume that. Why? What are you planning?"

"What am I...?" She was throwing me off. Maybe intentionally... probably. "Well, I don't know, Susan. The man just died a few hours ago, and we spoke to each other over his dead body. Why else would you be here?"

She seemed to consider; though, if she was looking for an actual answer or an insulting retort, I wasn't certain. Finally she tilted her head. "Mr. Beaker died by choking on a white chocolate cranberry scone earlier this afternoon in the middle of the celebratory launch of Black Bear Roaster's newest espresso."

I waited for her to continue, to ask a question or reveal some twist. She didn't. She continued to stare at me expectantly.

"Yes. I was there. Remember?"

Her growl was so low I almost thought Watson was back. "No need to be petulant."

"I'm not trying to be, Officer Green, but I don't understand where you're going with this."

"I'm simply asking if you would agree with that statement."

I sensed a trap, but I couldn't determine exactly where it was laid. I nodded, slowly, though even as I did, it felt like the wrong thing to do. "Yes. I would agree. I suppose."

"You suppose?" She straightened, and sure enough, unless I was mistaken, I heard an audible snap of the trap closing around my ankle. "Why do you say that? Is there some alternative reality that occurred that the rest of the coffee shop missed?"

The challenge in her tone was nearly enough to make me repeat what I just theorized as a possibility with Leo. Nearly. I matched her posture, straightening, then smoothed out my skirt. The motion didn't feel nearly as effective as Susan adjusting her holster, but still. "You tell me, Officer Green. If Eustace Beaker choked to death on a scone, why are you here? I didn't force-feed it to him."

"There was a witness saying that you overheard an altercation between the deceased and Carla Beaker." She kept her tone utterly flat.

I wasn't quick enough to disguise my flinch, and Susan's eyes narrowed.

Someone had noticed me eavesdropping? Maybe Myrtle Bantam.

The second the option flitted through my mind, I cast it away. She'd been in the bathroom. There hadn't been anyone else in the hallway.

That only left one option. Eustace must have mentioned to Carla that he'd seen me in the hall.

"Carla asked you to come here?"

It was Susan's turn to flinch.

Bingo.

Susan considered for a second. When she spoke,

her voice was pure, cold authority. "Just because family members argue right before death, doesn't mean there's foul play. No one needed to ask me to come here, Winifred. It's no secret that you love nothing more than snooping where your nose doesn't belong. It would be just like you to blow a tragic, yet accidental, death out of proportion and only cause more injury to the bereaved. I'm simply dropping by to make sure you don't have any of those notions in that fuzzy red head of yours."

Fuzzy? I bristled at the term. My hair was most definitely not fuzzy.

That wasn't the point. Good grief, that wasn't the point.

"Hello?" A voice broke the tension, along with the opening of the front door.

"One second, I'll be right there." I raised my voice but then lowered it again as I addressed Susan. "Katie and I are doing interviews to replace Sammy. It sounds like they are arriving. Do you need more of my time?"

"No. Definitely not. I don't have any questions for you. There's nothing to figure out." Susan stood, smoothed out her slacks, and once more readjusted her gun. And again, I had to admit that she was much more effective at that gesture than I was.

"Please don't make yourself a nuisance, Fred. I know that's a full-time job, but prove to me that you can do it, for once."

Before I could think of a retort, thankfully, she turned and walked away.

I took another second or two before stepping out to greet whoever had arrived for the first interview. I wasn't sure what was going on, but there was no doubt Carla had asked Susan to come speak to me. Or had at least mentioned she was worried about what I would do.

I'd already been thinking Eustace might not have choked. The possibility sounded absurd, enough so I truly might have pushed the possibility from my mind.

All chances of that had just flown out the window.

FOUR

"I didn't realize this was a cook-your-own-food kind of steak place." I stared down the long grill that filled up most of the narrow room. I'd never seen anything like it. It was like Katie's bakery counter, except instead of being topped with marble, it was one huge flaming grill with room on all four sides for people to stand and cook their chosen pieces of meat. "Actually, I didn't even know this sort of place existed anywhere. And that's saying something, since I grew up in the Midwest."

Branson flashed his movie-star smile as he held up his thick elk steak with a pair of metal tongs. "When you suggested meeting at Prime Slice, I didn't think about you never having eaten here before. The waitress did say they could cook the steaks for us if we want."

"Not on your life. I'm new enough in town to know that any choice I make in public affects my reputation. I'm not going to be known as the girl who's too good to cook her own steak."

Already the heat from the grill was getting to me, and I used one hand to pull my hair over my shoulders in an attempt to cool myself down. And I had actually taken the time to do more with my hair than simply run a brush through it. That would teach me. Taking another set of tongs, I lifted my filet cut of bison and placed it on the grill with a flourish. I was of two minds. On the one hand, the restaurant concept was a fun idea, something different than normal. But on the other, the steaks weren't any cheaper than at a five-star steakhouse, and I could've cooked for less money at home.

Branson followed my lead and finally lowered his steak to the grill as well, then ran his fingers through his thick black hair. The locks fell perfectly back into place as his bright green eyes sparkled at me through the waves of heat wafting between us.

Literal waves of heat—from the grill. Not metaphorical.

Although, maybe those were there too. I couldn't tell. Goodness knew, I was a nervous wreck, but at that moment I was more irritated at him for being so stinking pretty than anything else. Branson Wexler looked like he was shooting a commercial for the place, while I needed someone to hand me a paper towel to mop the sweat off my forehead.

"At least we don't have to bake our own potatoes." He reached down and slid a tray of seasoning between us and began to salt his steak. "I do love a woman who wants steak and potatoes, though." His eyes flashed again. "Did I mention how beautiful you are tonight? That sapphire blouse is really a great color on you."

"You did, when I arrived. Thank you." I shifted and looked away, grateful for the distraction of the spices to have something to do with my hands. I grabbed one of the bottles—I thought it was pepper. The blouse had been Katie's contribution to this reconciliatory date. She'd insisted I wear something jewel-toned instead of one of my preferred earthy colors.

Branson reached out and slid his hand over mine, forcing me to pause in my pepper seasoning. "If you keep going, you're going to sneeze with every bite you take."

Sure enough, I hadn't even realized I'd fairly encrusted the steak in the stuff.

He let his hand linger on mine for a few moments. "Don't worry, if it's too spicy, I'll share mine." His thumb moved on the back of my hand in what might have been a caress, or simply an unconscious twitch, before he released me.

I gulped and then traded it for the salt.

There had to be something to say. *Something*.

We'd been on a few dates before, but that had been months ago. Somehow, I was more nervous than our first one. "How was your trip?"

"Fine. Productive as always." He shrugged in his easy way and then, as usual when I brought up his constant quick trips, shifted the topic. "Thanks for agreeing to go on another date with me, Fred. I was afraid I'd screwed up any chance I had with you when everything went down with the bird club in January."

My next flash of irritation had nothing to do with him being prettier than me, and it helped. I switched saltshaker for the tongs and shook them in his direction. "You know, for as smooth as you are, I'd think you'd know better than to remind a woman of how bossy and controlling you can be."

"I was just doing my job, Fred."

"Really? I thought we'd come to an agreement since then that you can't tell me who I can or can't speak to if I have questions about a murder, or anything else for that matter."

"We did. *After* that case." He grinned. "And I've stuck to that since, haven't I?"

I set the tongs back down without using them before I smacked him in the head. Could you get in trouble for assaulting a police sergeant with cooking utensils while on a date with said sergeant? "And again, you surprise me. Is this arrogant tone of voice meant to be charming?"

He propped his hip on the counter bordering the grill, folded his arms, and all the while his smug smile stayed firmly in place. "You looked nervous. That's not fun, and I don't like seeing you uncomfortable. At least if you're irritated, you're more sure of yourself."

"Well that's just..." His meaning sank in, and I wasn't certain whether I was more tempted to smack him harder with the tongs or laugh. "You're irritating me on purpose, trying to make me feel at ease?"

"Depends..." He cocked an eyebrow. "Did it work?"

I didn't even have to consider. "Yes. But if you try to arrest me when I shove your face on the grill, I can promise you there will never be another date. Ever."

"See that? You're already talking about another date." He looked like he was struggling not to laugh.

"When you insisted on meeting here instead of having me pick you up, I figured my chances were slim."

I glowered at him. "Your chances *are* slim." I managed to keep a straight face for about three seconds and then laughed. He was good. I had to give him that. The irritation had faded, leaving me feeling at ease.

When I'd arrived in town last winter, the furthest thing from my mind had been dating, or men. In fact, they'd been on the strictly do-not-attempt list. Yet, there I was, despite all of that, on a date with a police sergeant. And possibly having feelings for a park ranger.

Maybe I was the one who needed a browbeating with the tongs.

Wisely, he changed the subject again, motioning to our steaks. "Probably time to flip them over. If you coat the other side with a thick layer of salt, it might just even out." He smiled teasingly, then bit his lower lip, giving him an air of innocence—which was most definitely not a trustworthy expression—before grinning fully once more. "I do know you make a delicious grilled cheese, but I am curious about your other cooking skills." He held up a hand. "Not that I judge a woman by her homemaking abilities. I'm a feminist, after all."

I wasn't exactly sure how true that was. He kept sending me mixed messages on that, along with everything else. Although I'd never gotten the sense that the mixed signals were due to me being a woman—if I had, I would never have gone out on a date with him to begin with. But still, I wasn't sure. Not sure about much regarding Branson Wexler, if I was being honest with myself. Which… maybe was why I'd said yes to going on another date.

I shoved that thought aside. I hated to think what that said about me.

We finished cooking our steaks in relative ease, despite the increasing heat, and from the looks he gave me, maybe not all of it was simply from the grill.

As if by magic, as soon as we sat down with our steaks at the table, the waitress arrived with baked potatoes and all the toppings, cornbread casserole, and roasted brussels sprouts with candied bacon.

The combined aromas were a little slice of heaven. I licked my lips to keep from adding salivating to the list of bodily functions that were most definitely on the ruin-date list.

Branson cut into his elk steak, took a bite, and gave a groan that was a little bit too exaggerated to be construed as anything other than flirtatious. "Now that's amazing. I'm quite the grill master, if I do say so myself." He winked. "I confess, I've been here a couple of times. Prime Slice has one of the best chocolate cakes around. Second only to Katie's, I'm sure."

I'd said yes to the date with Branson because... well... I *wanted* to go on a date with Branson, despite myself, but I'd also been looking for a segue on to other topics. And that moment might be as close as I could hope to get. I'd just been about to pop my first bite of steak into my mouth, but I lowered it back down to the plate and leaned forward. "Speaking of dessert, I've found myself wondering about scones over the past couple of days."

Branson's eyes narrowed, and his tone grew wary. "Seriously, Fred? Is that why you finally said yes to going on a date with me again?"

"No. Not at all." He looked hurt. Genuinely. Without thinking I reached out and placed my hand over his. "I'm sorry."

He studied me for a second, seemed convinced, and then smiled again before taking another bite.

I released his hand and followed suit. I nearly choked. Both the salt and pepper, and some other herb I'd bathed my poor bison in, filled up all my senses in an attempt to strangle me. I washed it down with a quick gulp of water, then had to thump my chest once before clearing my throat.

Branson stared at me, and though he managed to keep from laughing, the amusement in his tone was nearly tangible. "You okay?"

I nodded, sucked in a breath, and managed words. "Yes. But I don't think I quite qualify as grill master. Although, if your steak is lacking any seasoning, you can borrow some of mine. It seems I dumped an entire spice cabinet on this thing."

"We can ask them to cook you another one."

"Absolutely not. It was my own fault. And this poor little buffalo shouldn't have died in vain. I'll just scrape off what I can and douse it with steak sauce." I forced a smile. "At least there's cake."

"Here, we'll split." Branson cut his steak in half and slid a portion onto my plate. "At the end, we'll each get our own huge piece of chocolate cake to make up for it. None of that splitting mumbo jumbo."

And with that suggestion, impossibly, the man got even better-looking. "Thank you for the steak." I cut into it, hesitated, and focused up at him once more. "But... speaking of cake, and desserts..."

He let out what sounded like a frustrated laugh

and threw up his hands. "Oh, for crying out loud. You really can't help yourself, can you?"

I shrugged in way of apology. "No, I don't think I can."

Branson set down his fork, folded his hands on the tabletop, and leveled his stare. "Okay, how about this, just get it all out at once, and then we can move on and actually have a date instead of an interrogation. How does that sound?"

"Marvelous, actually." I followed his example, folding my hands, and shimmied in my chair with pleasure. Finally, I might be able to get somewhere. I'd been stewing over my conversation with Susan for the past two days. Not to mention practically driving Katie crazy as I refused to talk about anything else. "I suppose Officer Green mentioned her conversation with me?"

"She did." He nodded. "She was under the impression that you might believe Mr. Beaker died of foul play?"

I studied him for a moment, attempting to judge his reaction. "I think it's a possibility."

"Okay, why?" No smirk, no sound of disbelief, not even the hint of judgment. Maybe he was faking it, but even so, I appreciated his seriousness.

"From what I witnessed in the little time I was

there, and then from what I've heard about him outside of the coffee shop, the man was a fairly horrible human being. Not a murderer or anything, but it seems like he was unkind to nearly everyone who crossed his path. The type of man who might have a lot of enemies."

Branson considered, then gave another slow nod. "Okay, but how? From your own report, you saw the man choking on a scone and then rush off toward the restroom. Carla found him dead in the hallway mere moments later."

Again, it seemed like he was genuinely asking.

"I don't know exactly. The only thing I can think of is that his scone was poisoned." I held up a hand. "Yes, I know that it would've had to have been a fairly fast-acting poison to have had any effect. Trust me, Katie's been on a Google binge to convince me of just that. So I don't know. Maybe poison, maybe something else. I just know that it seemed entirely too convenient from all I witnessed from him in that short time, being absolutely horrible to so many people, for him to drop dead out of the blue without some assistance."

"But, Fred, again, you said so yourself. Eustace Beaker was a miserable, mean man. He was awful to everyone, all the time. We all have to die at some point. It would've been much more unlikely for him to do so after being kind."

He had a point. One that I'd thought of several times. And one that had almost convinced me to let it go. "I can't explain it. I don't want to call it a gut feeling because that sounds crazy, but... well... it's a gut feeling."

"Fred." This time Branson reached over and took my hand, and he sounded apologetic more than judgmental or like he was simply humoring me. "The coroner determined his cause of death was asphyxiation by choking. The man's getting buried tomorrow. What do you want me to do?"

I hadn't heard that bit of coroner information, at least not officially. Maybe I was being ridiculous. "Did anyone test the scone?"

"I'm sure there are samples of it." He sighed, sounding tired. "But such a tox screen wasn't ordered. The cause of death was cut and dry."

I opened my mouth to protest but didn't have an argument to offer.

Luckily, Branson cut me off before he realized that fact as he lifted his free hand. "But... how about this. Would you be satisfied if I go in tomorrow and see if they indeed have a sample of the scone, and if so, I'll have them test it? Will that work?"

"Yes. That will work." A wave of relief washed over me that I hadn't felt since Mr. Beaker's death. "Thank you."

He smiled, still handsome and charming, but now back to easy and warm once more. "Now... can we return to date conversation?"

"Sure." I smiled at him, appreciating that he seemed willing to listen to me when he hadn't been several months ago. Sometimes second chances were warranted. "That sounds good."

"Finally." He reached across the table, took my hand once more, and held it lightly. "There's been something I've been dying to ask you all night."

My heart rate sped up at his suddenly serious tone. "Okay..."

"If I..." He swallowed, glanced away nervously and then back again, and started over. "If I said you had a beautiful body, would you hold it against me?"

My jaw fell open.

His lips twitched.

I jerked my hand away and swatted his shoulder with a laugh. "Shut up! You are ridiculous!"

And miraculously, for the rest of dinner, there was only laughter, easy conversation, and cake. I didn't think of Eustace Beaker again until my drive home.

FIVE

The soft yellow of the sunrise brought to mind the hue of Katie's lemon bars. I watched from the drift-wood bench on the porch of my log cabin as the morning stars began to fade from view above the mountain peaks. The sun had yet to crest on the horizon, leaving the surrounding forest shadowed and dense. Only a quarter mile away was a McMansion subdivision, then the smaller neighborhoods that led into Estes Park.

With every day that passed, I felt more and more at home, tucked away in the woods. I was a long way from the city girl I'd always been. Though, I had a feeling the transition to who I was going to become had barely started. Every once in a while, just how much my life had altered crashed around me, leaving me feeling anxious and somewhat disoriented. But more than anything? It was exciting. I got to be someone new. Maybe the Fred I was always meant to be.

A motion called to me from the corner of my eye, pulling me out of my overanalyzing state.

"Oh no you don't."

Watson halted at the edge of the two steps that led into the yard, casting a quasi-guilt-ridden, part-defiant glance my way.

"Yes, *you*, mister." I'd had both hands wrapped around my coffee mug for warmth, but I shook a finger at him. "We've had this talk before. I know you think everything you see is food, but half the things in those woods see you that way as well. If you want to go down there, we get a leash."

His ears flicked back, and he chuffed out an annoyed breath, considering the clearing in front of the house once more, as if debating how disobedient he wanted to be. After a stubborn couple of seconds, he slunk back and folded himself at my feet, offering me one more judgmental, withering stare, before closing his eyes.

"I know. I can tell you're thinking I'm crazy." I pulled my grandmother's old quilt tighter around me, snuggled into it, and then cupped the mug of coffee in my hands once more. "You're not wrong. I light the fire at the bookshop so it's a billion degrees, and then I wake up before dawn and come sit on the porch and shiver. Insane, I know. But I couldn't sleep any longer."

I waited for some response. Another chuff, yawn, or even an opportune moment of flatulence. Ever the obstinate one, Watson feigned sleep.

Surprisingly, falling asleep hadn't been a problem. Somehow, I'd managed to not overanalyze the date with Branson. Even the brief goodbye kiss we'd shared as we'd gone our separate ways after dinner. Although, that had been part of what had woken me up. The kiss had been nice, comforting in a way. Strange in another.

Was a kiss supposed to be nice?

I'd really thought that aspect of my life was over. Maybe that was silly. I'd gotten divorced when I was thirty-two. And I was going to be thirty-nine in a couple of weeks. Did I really expect to have finished the relationship portion of my life in my early thirties? Had I really expected to spend the rest of my life alone? Alone, but not lonely? Had I expected it, wanted it, or thought that was all I could have?

Regardless, it was safer.

Branson... Well, he wasn't safe. Actually, he felt

safe. He said he would never hurt me, and though there was very little I understood about the man, that part I could feel. He wouldn't. Ever. But the rest? I couldn't get a good gauge on who he was. Maybe that attracted me to him as much as his beautiful face. Surely that was a problem.

A groan cut the quiet of the morning. I glanced down at Watson, who peered back up at me as if annoyed I'd disrupted his fake nap.

It seemed I'd been the one who groaned.

And rightly so. Good grief. Much too heavy thoughts for such a pretty, barely-started morning.

I shoved Branson and possible romance out of my mind.

Leo flitted through for a second, but I chased him away as well.

Instead, Eustace Beaker strolled into my thoughts.

There. That was much preferable. Murder was a lot easier to handle than the possibility of relationships.

I wasn't going to think about that inclination, which was probably a problem, as well.

But murder? Maybe I really was seeing things that I wanted to be there, to avoid such confusion as relationships. Even though Branson hadn't said he thought I was crazy, it was clear he was simply humoring me about getting the scone tested.

Eustace had choked. It happened. All the time. And considering the texture of Carla's scones, it was a small miracle it hadn't happened on a daily basis since she'd opened her coffee shop. How many times over the past several months had I thought they were little more than choking hazards? And yet, here I was, proven correct, but now skeptical.

Branson had been right. From what I'd observed and heard about Eustace, he was rather miserable to everyone all the time. It would've been much more shocking if he had died after a moment of *not* being awful to someone. But... if anybody seemed a candidate for having enough enemies that one of them wanted you dead, Eustace Beaker had the perfect resume.

His funeral was later that afternoon. Part of me wanted to attend, just to observe, see who was gathered in the crowd, secretly rejoicing. Although chances were high there would be more than one of those individuals present.

I wasn't going to go. It wouldn't be appropriate. I didn't know him, didn't like what I did know of him, and if Carla had sicced Susan on me to warn me off, then showing up wouldn't be a good idea.

And... maybe I really was searching for things that weren't there. Maybe some unflattering part of me was enjoying solving murders just a little too much, and now was looking for them where there was nothing to find.

Watson sighed a long, contented doggy sigh and stretched as the sun finally broke the peaks and filtered down onto the porch, offering him some warmth.

I'd brought *The Chipmunk Chronicles*, the Estes Park newspaper, on the porch with me, but it had been too dark to read and I hadn't wanted to turn onto the porch light. But I reached for it then, trading its location on the small log table with my coffee mug, then flipped through it and opened to Eustace's obituary. I'd read it the night before, but wanted to again.

It was written by Athena Rose, and I could almost hear her cultured voice read it to me over my shoulder.

Eustace Beaker, aged seventy-six years. Survived by wife, Ethel, son, Jonathan, daughter-in-law, Carla, and grandson, Maverick. Eustace Beaker built a life of success and privilege. He devoted his existence to shaping Estes Park and the surrounding community in the fashion he believed best for those of the town.

Mr. Beaker used his resources to accumulate real estate and businesses, and influence the town government, organizations, and ordinances. As the chairman of the town council for the past three decades, there is not a solitary aspect of Estes Park that has not been touched by Eustace's influence. He was passionate in his beliefs and standards, and assisted in helping others rise to meet those expectations. There will be a vast emptiness in Eustace Beaker's absence. He was a force of will who refused to be denied, and the town will not be the same without him.

If I hadn't met Athena a few days before, I might have read the obituary in a much different light. I was sure of that actually. In many ways it was flattering. It told of a man who was powerful, in control, passionate about the town, and worked tirelessly to shape it the way he saw fit. But Athena's distaste for the man was apparent. As was my own. Knowing that lent a much different filter to her writing. One that was barely disguised. A person didn't even need to read between the lines, not really, to see that she was basically calling him a power-hungry, controlling tyrant, who abused his influence and privilege to be little more than a dictator of his kingdom.

I traced Athena's name with my fingernail, considering.

If Eustace had been murdered, given her history and her position at the paper, Athena might be able to provide quite the exhaustive list of people who could have wanted to speed along the absence Eustace left behind.

I waited until midmorning to leave Katie alone at the Cozy Corgi. There seemed a lull after the breakfast rush in the bakery, then business started again around noon. Book sales were always slow in the morning and tended to pick up in the afternoon when tourists began to stroll lazily through the shops after their morning hikes.

The offices of *The Chipmunk Chronicles*, though small, were surprisingly modern and sleek. The outside was done in the typical river rock and dark wood siding that much of the town had, but the interior seemed to be transported from somewhere else. Not at all the quaint little village feel, like I'd expected.

The receptionist cast a quizzical glance at Watson when I requested to speak to Athena but didn't offer commentary on his presence. Most places in Estes were dog friendly, but perhaps she felt a trail of corgi hair didn't really suit the ambience of the newspaper.

Little did she know that his presence didn't affect that fact all that much. There weren't enough lint rollers in existence to keep my outfits from dispersing corgi fluff wherever I went.

"Fred!" Athena offered a welcoming smile as she turned from her computer to find Watson and me at her door. She swiveled around and flickered those french-tipped fingers our way. "And Watson. What a nice surprise." Though she didn't stand, she offered an outstretched hand in my direction.

I took it, giving a squeeze before I sat down in the chair by her desk. "Thanks for letting us drop in like this. I probably should've called, but sometimes, when I get something in my mind, I have a hard time shaking it and act without thinking." True enough, but I'd also discovered that when I wanted to get the most honest answers from someone, it was best to not give them time to prepare.

"Goodness, no. It's not a bother at all. Quite nice actually. As you can imagine, there aren't too many people who drop by to talk about obituaries. And when they do, it's never a pleasant meeting." She straightened the golden purple scarf at her throat. "I do wish I had dog treats or something. I hate not being able to offer such a cute visitor anything."

At the word "treats," Watson perked up, and gave a bunny bounce on his front paws.

"She said she *doesn't* have one of those, Watson." I patted his head. "Breathe, buddy."

Her dark eyes widened, and she winced. "Oh, I'm so sorry. That word probably isn't a very good one to say, is it?"

"It can get you in trouble. I'm afraid one of the things Watson and I have in common is that we share a sweet tooth." I cast him a sidelong glance. "If we don't mention it again, he'll forget in a couple of minutes. Well, no, he won't forget, but that look of frantic desperation on his face will slowly transition to one of forlorn betrayal."

Athena chuckled and smiled as she settled back in her seat. "I knew I liked you. And your little dog. I wish I had brought Pearl in with me today. But it's not allowed." Her head twitched slightly as if experiencing a new thought. One of her long nails tapped the arm of her chair. "Now that I think about it, since the paper will soon be under new management, maybe Pearl can join me before long. That would definitely make my days better."

"Oh, that would be nice. Did the paper sell?"

She cocked an eyebrow. "Not exactly. The owner just passed. Which I figured is why you're here." There was the slightest hint of humor in her voice.

"Am I that obvious?"

"Yes. And no." She gestured toward the folded-up paper in my hand. "I would imagine you read the obituary, the funeral is today, and you do have a reputation in town already."

I tried to determine if there was judgment in her tone, but I didn't think so. Though not necessarily approval either. Either way, it saved time, and I preferred being straightforward whenever possible. "You caught me. I did come to talk about the obituary, or about the man, more specifically. Though I didn't realize Eustace owned the paper."

"Darling, the only person who owns more in town is your stepfather. But two more different men there couldn't be." Athena leaned forward, snagged a small notepad and pen from her desk, then seemed to think better of it and replaced them. "I take it, by your presence here, you suspect foul play?"

She was a quick one, and direct as well. It seemed my initial impression of her the other day had been on point. "The police think I'm grasping at straws, to say the least, but I can't help but think that's a strong possibility."

"I'm sure it doesn't hurt that you're seeing someone on the force. That's an inside track most of us don't have."

Not a day went by where it wasn't made overtly clear that I was building a new life in a small town. One where everyone knew everything at all times. Though I had no idea where things were going with Branson, if anywhere beyond a few dates and maybe some more kisses, there was no reason to clarify that, so I let it be. "I'm not sure if that gives what the police see as my harebrained theory any more credence than if you would've come up with it." I didn't want to talk about Branson or the police, however. "But I wanted to pick your brain. Especially after reading your obituary and our conversation the other day."

She smiled, her violet-red lips glistening in a nearly sinister way. "Hoping I'll provide you with a list of suspects?"

On second thought, she was a little more direct than was comfortable. I attempted a laugh, trying to lighten the mood. "I wasn't planning on putting it quite that bluntly."

She waved me off. "Oh, Fred, when you get to be

my age, there's no time for subtlety." She shrugged one thin shoulder. "But I'm afraid I won't be of much use. There are technically six thousand people in town. Although, that number fluctuates greatly between the summer and winter months and those who are permanent and part-time residents. I imagine the list I would provide would be around six thousand people long. Not very helpful at all."

I waited for a laugh, some punch line.

But though her eyes twinkled, her expression stayed serious.

"So everyone hated the man?"

"Everyone who met him. Except his family." She blinked rapidly, those false eyelashes attempting a look of innocence. "Although, even members of his family hated the man, as I figure you could imagine."

"Carla?" Her name slipped through my lips without any forethought, and I wished I could suck it back in. I liked Athena, quite a bit, though she was making me more uncomfortable than she had when we'd first met. She didn't strike me as a gossip, but who could say. There were enough hard feelings between Carla and myself without it getting back to her that I brought her up in connection with her father-in-law's death.

Athena didn't miss a beat. "I don't know your

story, Winifred. I do know that you're divorced, but I haven't been privy to the how and why. So I can't say what your experience was with a father-in-law. But let me tell you, an overbearing father-in-law can make life just as miserable as an abusive husband." Her expression softened. "I'm not, however, saying that Carla had anything to do with Eustace dying. I'm simply stating that as far as who might want to have a Eustace Beaker-sized hole in their life, that list is endless. I imagine it would be impossible to meet the man without hating him. So, really... the question isn't who hated him enough to kill him; it's, of all the people who hated him, who might be willing to kill."

The conversation with Athena was going in such a different direction than what I'd anticipated. I figured she'd laugh me off. And even if she didn't, I most definitely couldn't have predicted such a response. "To be frank, I only met the man that once. And while I didn't come away with a good impression, I can't say I'd noticed enough to hate him."

She gave another shrug, completely unconcerned, and once more settled back in her chair, this time folding her hands in her lap. "That's only because you didn't have long enough to know him."

I hesitated, examining the implication of her words. She hadn't been subtle in her implication to begin with, so I followed her lead. "And you? Did you hate Eustace Beaker?"

She hesitated as well, though her smile returned, and strangely, it seemed approving. "Hate isn't something a person should give in to, Fred. We should fight against it, rise above it. Seek forgiveness and find a way to cleanse such darkness from our souls." Her gaze held mine, unashamed and unflinching. "But yes. I hated Eustace Beaker. Completely."

I flinched, enough that Watson glanced up at me in concern.

Athena blinked, but didn't look away. "Don't let me down, Fred. I know I'm the one working for the paper, and that you're not a reporter, but go ahead. Do your follow-up."

I couldn't stand being told what to do. By anyone. It was probably at the top of my list of things I detested. But Athena's demand felt different somehow. "Did you kill Eustace?"

And still she smiled.

Athena didn't answer for several heartbeats. For a moment, I thought I was about to get a confession. Finally, her smile faltered. "No. I didn't. But I'm glad he's dead."

I let out a breath I hadn't been aware I was

holding and relaxed somewhat. "Do you know who did?"

"If you ever leave that bookshop of yours, you'd make a great career here at the paper." She studied me for a moment and then shook her head. "Darling, as far as I know, the only thing that happened was a miracle taking the form of a scone."

SIX

"Katie Pizzolato, I can't believe you." I'd just entered the bakery after locking up the bookstore downstairs and gaped at the dough Katie was cutting into pie-shaped slices.

Leo chuckled softly from his kneeling position on the floor as he stroked an utterly content Watson.

For her part, Katie made another slice and then looked up, her brown eyes full of innocence. "What? You've seen me bake before, nothing new."

"Scones? You're actually making scones at a time like this? On the very day Eustace Beaker was buried?" Though I'm certain it made me a horrible person, it was taking all my willpower not to laugh.

She shrugged. "It's not my fault I've had a strange craving for them for days. I suppose it's because you won't quit talking about them." The corner of her lips twitched. "And why shouldn't I make them? I can promise that nobody will choke on mine."

The room went still, the three of us looked back and forth at each other, and then Leo threw back his head and laughed, causing Watson to flinch.

And that was the end of it. Katie lost control and began to laugh as well, and then I threw in the towel and gave up any semblance of self-control.

We laughed until tears rolled, and I was nearly doubled over, hands on my knees and battling for breath.

After several moments, and for the first time since Watson had met Leo, he gave us a condemning glare and scurried away from Leo's affection to shelter underneath the table along the far wall. His condemnation only made the three of us laugh harder.

After a while, I managed to catch my breath and wiped my eyes. "This officially makes us absolutely horrible people. You both realize that, right?"

Leo nodded, but hadn't managed to quit chuckling.

"Maybe so, but we'll be well-fed and satisfied horrible people." Katie sniffed and motioned toward two bowls containing unrolled-out dough. "This recipe is hands down the best scone recipe around. Completely simple, and utterly customizable. I'm making mine plain and just doing a quick sugar glaze on top after they're baked. But you two can pick out your own ingredients if you want, and I'll mix them in."

"Just because they're made to order doesn't mean this isn't the tackiest thing any of us have ever done." Despite my protests, I wasn't overly concerned. It wasn't as if the rest of the town were there to overhear.

"So..." Katie cocked an eyebrow. "You *don't* want yours with chocolate, pecans, and drizzled in caramel?"

"Never mind, sign me up for being a truly horrible person." I smacked the marble countertop. "You had me at chocolate."

Leo stood and lifted a hand in the air. "And this horrible person wants white chocolate chips and dried cherries, with powdered sugar on top."

"You two are so easily corruptible." Katie winked and got to work pouring copious amounts of chocolate chips into one of the bowls.

No wonder I loved my best friend.

After a few seconds, Leo joined her behind the counter and helped himself to the supplies and added his own ingredients. "Did you guys settle on an assistant after the interviews the other day?"

I halted at his question, surprised that Katie hadn't already filled him in. Maybe there wasn't a romance growing between them.

"No. None of them felt right." Katie sighed as she folded toasted pecans into my batter. "Although I'm not sure if anyone will be right. I know Sammy and I were starting to struggle toward the end, but it just seems wrong replacing her."

I didn't feel quite so strongly as Katie about that, but none of the people who we'd interviewed had clicked with me, either. "Well, we will need to pick someone soon. We can't keep going like we are. Not with the season picking up. But I bet there will be a spike in Carla's business for the next few weeks after the drama, so that might give us a little breathing room."

"That's good for Carla. I'm glad of that." Katie shook her head, a shadow flitting over her expression. "People are strange creatures, aren't they? You'd think having someone die eating your scones would make people run away, but instead they want a piece of the drama. Exactly what happened here after Sammy was killed, and... everything else..."

When the truth about Katie's past had emerged

after Sammy's murder, our already busy bakery had been filled to overflowing for weeks. It had been a bittersweet time for Katie. Finally feeling known and accepted, but also a bit like a circus freak on display. As that had died down, though, she'd become brighter and happier than I'd ever seen her, which, given her already cheerful disposition, was saying something. And nice to watch.

Leo appeared to pick up on her mood as well, but for once, didn't seem sure what to say.

I wasn't either, so I opted for distraction. "I hadn't gotten to talk to you since I spoke with Athena. But it was quite the experience. She is one intense lady."

Katie latched on to the topic as she began to roll out my batch of scones. "I've noticed she and Paulie hang out quite a bit. She'd have to be somewhat intense to be able to do that successfully."

That was a true story. If for no other reason than having the ability to put up with his two insane corgis. "She actually came out and stated plainly that she hated Eustace. That she was glad he was dead."

Both Katie and Leo paused and looked up at me in unison, but it was Leo who spoke. "Are you thinking she had something to do with it?"

"I'm not sure. I don't think so." I reached out and

snagged a bit of dough and popped it into my mouth. I knew it wasn't recommended to do such things, but I couldn't help myself. Katie had the same proclivity, so she never got on me for it. Scone dough wasn't as scrumptious as cookie dough, but good, nonetheless. "Although if Athena did, just coming out and saying it would be one way to throw me off."

"You still think he was murdered?" There wasn't judgment in Leo's tone, which I appreciated.

"I can't shake that feeling. Branson agreed to have the scone tested for poison, if they still have a sample."

"Then we'll know soon enough." Katie returned to the new dough and began to slice it into wedges. "I can't imagine how Athena would've pulled it off, though. I mean, she and Paulie were there before we were, but how would she have access to Carla's scones?"

"I was wondering the same thing. Plus, how would she know which scone Eustace would choose." I nearly stopped myself from saying my next thought, and if it had been with anyone else, I would've. "Athena brought up what a horrible father-in-law Eustace must've been..."

Again, Katie and Leo looked at me in unison, and once more, Leo was the one who spoke, though he sounded hesitant. "She thinks *Carla* might have killed Eustace?"

I shrugged. "She definitely didn't say it in that many words, but it seemed she was raising the possibility."

There was a loud clunk as Katie cut through one of the pecans. She cleared her throat, but didn't say anything.

Leo and I exchanged glances, and I focused on Katie. "Your thoughts are so loud, you might as well say them."

Katie looked up, like she'd been caught, and then sighed. "I don't think Carla would do that. I mean, we all know she has a temper, but she's not a murderer."

"I would agree"—I held Katie's gaze—"but that's not all you were thinking."

Another sigh. "Well, it was miserable working at Black Bear Roaster, even though I didn't do it for very long. Carla was not pleasant to work for, but Eustace was a nightmare. Not that he came by that often, but when he did, he was ranting and raving, bossing everyone around, including Carla. And he treated us baristas as if we were dirt under his nails." She shook her head, her spiral curls dancing above her shoulders. "But that doesn't mean she killed him.

I just don't see it. It's not who she is. Plus, she just had a baby. She wouldn't kill Maverick's grandfather."

It was a good point. Although, if the man was that horrible, maybe she felt she was doing her son a favor, not having to grow up with such a mean grandfather. Still, I couldn't picture Carla committing murder either. "You're probably right, and maybe that wasn't Athena's intention. Goodness knows I can't get a good read on her. But she seems blunt enough that if she thought Carla had killed Eustace she might've just come out and said it."

We were silent for a while, each lost in thought, the only sounds filling the room was Katie rolling out Leo's mixture of scones and Watson licking his paws from across the room.

Finally, Leo cleared his throat. "Anyway, I don't suppose there's any point speculating, at least not until we find out if the scone was poisoned or not."

"I guess you're right." I forced a lightheartedness into my voice I didn't quite feel. "Besides, even if the scone was poisoned, it's not my job to figure out who did it, right?"

Katie and Leo both smirked, and this time it was Katie who spoke. "Right, because *that* would stop you." She finished loading the scones onto the baking sheets and checked her watch. "But you're running late, aren't you?"

I looked at my cell. "I am." I slid the phone back into the pocket of my skirt and patted my thigh, calling Watson over to me. "Are you sure you two don't mind helping us tonight?"

"Are you kidding?" Katie chuckled. "I love seeing your entire family together. It's better than watching a sitcom. I'll bring over the scones when they're finished baking. There'll be enough for everyone."

"I'll come with you, Fred. You're going to need as many hands working as possible." Leo started to walk around the counter.

I waved him off. "No. Stay with Katie, help her. Believe me, there'll be enough of us for a while. Besides, knowing my family, we'll spend a good hour debating what plan of action we should choose before we actually start any work. Plus, there will be pizza to order and that always takes a while to reach topping consensus."

Katie shook her head as if clearing a fog and glanced toward either side of the shop. "I am glad we avoided the Garble sisters taking over the candy stores, but I gotta say, it's going to be a trip having Verona and Zelda on one side, and Jonah and Noah on the other."

"Tell me about it." My stepsisters were twins, and they had married twin brothers. The shops on either side of the Cozy Corgi had been empty since I'd moved in, but now each set of twins was setting up shop. It was going to be a lot of family, a lot of the time. I loved them, but they were intense. "One thing's for sure, we're never going to be bored again."

"Bored?" Leo guffawed. "Fred, has there been one solitary moment where any of us have been bored since you moved to town?"

"He's not wrong. Even now, somebody chokes on a scone, and we're all thinking it's murder." Katie chuckled along. "You go on, Fred. We'll meet you there shortly."

All it took to get Watson ready to go was to mention my stepfather's name, Barry. He hurried out from under the table, darted toward the steps, then cast a longing glance at Leo. Poor little guy. He clearly was having a crisis of conscience leaving one love affair for the next.

Noticing, Leo waved him on. "I'll be there in a few minutes, little man. Go have fun."

And with that, Watson rushed down the steps and waited at the bottom, staring up at me in a manner that conveyed I was taking entirely too long.

"You're a mess, you know that?" I ruffled his fur

when I reached the bottom, eliciting one of his rare full-mouthed grins, and he pranced alongside me as I gathered up my purse and headed toward the front door. Considering we were going all of five feet, I didn't bother with his leash, and he stayed by my feet as I locked up.

The Garble sisters had owned the candy stores on either side of the bookshop. One of them had been a genuine candy store, the other had been an alternative health-food version and sold things that didn't come close to resembling candy. Verona and Zelda were taking over the one that had housed the actual candy store, which sat to the left of my shop. Their husbands were taking over the other. We were starting on my sisters' shop that evening.

"Fred, darling!" A happy screech greeted me as I turned from the Cozy Corgi. Before I could react, my tall, balding, nearly scarecrow-thin uncle threw open his arms in a flourish and wrapped me in a hug.

Watson took a couple steps back. Percival was always a little much for him to handle.

"Can you explain why the family got roped into clearing out the shops when your parents have more money than God?" Percival released me and held me at arm's length, lifting both his perfectly plucked eyebrows. "And on family dinner night as well."

"Always the gracious one, aren't you?" Gary, his linebacker of a husband tsked and squeezed my arm in greeting as Percival let me go. "Good to see you, as always, Fred." He grinned down at Watson and gave a wave of his large hand. "And you too, of course."

A couple of tourists squeezed past our small group, and then Percival slipped his arm through mine. "I'm so glad we're not the only ones running late. Although, the three of us—" His gaze flicked to Watson, then back up. "—four of us, I suppose... could go to the movies, send a text saying we got caught up, and be even later."

"Knock it off. How many times have Phyllis and Barry helped us?"

Before Percival could offer a smart-aleck comment to Gary, I jumped in, knowing that once they started bickering, we could be standing there for the next half hour. "Katie and Leo are inside right now, finishing up some freshly baked scones. I don't think you want to miss that."

"Scones!" Percival and Gary both reared back as they looked at me, and for once, Gary managed an expression just as dramatic as his husband's.

Percival laughed and clapped his hands together. "Oh my goodness, that is delicious, and somewhat scandalous, which makes it even *more* delicious." He cackled again. "Well, we'll have to toast them to old Eustace's memory."

Surprisingly, though he was typically the calming force, or at least the more socially appropriate one, Gary didn't bother to reprimand Percival's callous comment. It seemed there were two more people who weren't fans of the late Mr. Beaker.

"I don't really think that was what Katie had in mind." Despite my protestations, I couldn't keep the grin off my face. I started to motion toward the front door to suggest we go and start helping the others but paused as my attention was captured by the lettering over the window. With the brown paper taped over the inside, the scarlet script reading *Sinful Bites* almost looked like blood. Appropriate, in many ways. "Strange to think that this is all going to be something new, finally. I think part of me expected Opal and Iris to come back somehow."

"They almost did." Percival walked over, standing in front of the lettering as Gary joined Watson and me at the door. "Thank goodness Barry gave the Garble nieces a price they couldn't refuse. Who knows what life would've been like."

Before Gary or I could speculate, tires squealed, someone screamed, and the three of us whirled toward the street.

A silver Ford Contour cut across the opposite lane of traffic and zoomed toward us.

I reared back, trying to get out of the way, but my feet collided with Watson, tangled, and I stumbled backward, taking Watson down with me.

In a moment that seemed to take hours and yet was less than a heartbeat, I saw the world as if in slow motion as I fell. Tourists scattered. The old man behind the wheel, eyes wide, wild, and glassy. The silver car picking up speed and heading right at Percival.

There was a dark flash as Gary launched himself toward his husband, smashed into him, and then the car crashed through the window of Sinful Bites, erupting in an explosion of glass and bricks.

Everything was silent. Oddly so. The only sound was a ringing in my ears. For a second, or maybe much longer, I'm not sure, I couldn't figure out what I was seeing. Everything seemed upside down.

Then, I realized that's exactly what it was. Well, kind of. I was staring up at the bright blue sky, thick with white, cottony clouds. In front of it was the pitched roofline of the Cozy Corgi. I blinked, trying to make sense of this new perspective, when Watson's nose shoved against my cheek with a rough, wet nudge.

His whine broke through the reverberation in my ears, and he licked my face desperately.

"I'm okay. I'm okay." More out of the need to soothe him than anything else, I managed to touch him with one hand while slowly pushing myself to a sitting position with the other. At least, I thought I was okay. The fact that I wasn't entirely sure sent a shot of panic through me for Watson. I yanked him to me, pulling him onto my lap in a position he normally despised, but he didn't resist, just kept licking my face as my hands roamed over his body.

He was fine too. Watson was fine.

As Watson continued his inspection of me, I looked past him, to the car buried halfway inside Opal's old shop. The world still seemed frozen. And blurry. Sunlight caught the cloud of dust and particles of debris floating in the air, causing the scene to be hazy. Cars had come to a stop on the street, as had all the people scattered over the sidewalk.

And then, with a nearly audible click, the world began to move again, but this time at an accelerated pace. My mother rushed from the door of the candy shop, which had somehow remained intact. And then the rest of my family spilled out behind her.

She found me instantly and rushed to my side as I stood. "Fred, baby. Sweetheart. Are you okay?" Her hands traveled over my body just as mine had done to Watson.

I didn't resist her touch, but took a few steps toward the car, pulling her along with me as Barry and the others joined her. "Percival." I pointed at the rear end of the Ford Contour protruding over the sidewalk. "Percival and Gary. I think it hit... I think..." Still partially in a daze, I hurried around, the others following me, and from the other side, the people on the sidewalk rushed toward the epicenter as well.

I couldn't see them. Couldn't see either of them. What if they were underneath the car, or had been crushed against the building as the car had plowed through.

I hadn't been quick enough. Not even close. All I'd managed to do was trip over my dog.

As I rounded the back of the car, Gary was standing, pushing his tall frame up from the ground. I sucked in a breath at the sight of him, and then let out a cry when I saw him drop his hand and help Percival regain a standing position as well.

And then the two of them were surrounded by the family. Once more, hands everywhere, voices raised, and onslaughts of questions, exclamations, and assurances.

For once, Percival seemed speechless. His face was slack, and his eyes wide. There was a cut across his cheek, and scrapes over the back of his forearms.

Gary had similar injuries to his arms, and his pants were ripped, revealing marks from the sidewalk over his knee and down his shin.

Other than that, they seemed fine.

"What the...?" Percival blinked, shook his head, then winced. He stared at the car. "It tried to kill me." He gripped Gary's hand. "That car tried to kill me." He turned toward his husband. "You... you saved me."

"You're okay, baby. You're okay." Gary pulled Percival to him. "We're all okay."

Sirens sounded in the distance.

Percival pulled free, fury over his face. I'd never seen him look like that. He was nearly unrecognizable, such anger combined with the blood running over his cheek. He stomped toward the car, stepping over what was left of the lower portion of the wall and into the interior of the shop. "Who is this? I'm going to murder them for trying to kill us."

Gary hurried after him, begging him to calm down, to breathe. The rest of us followed.

I paused long enough to sweep Watson into my arms to keep his feet off the broken glass and sharp debris. He didn't resist, and I was once again reminded that my little man needed a diet.

From out of nowhere, Leo and Katie had joined us, and Leo lifted Watson from my arms. "Here. I've got him."

Watson squirmed, trying to get back to me, but I

refocused on my uncles, joining them beside the driver-side door as Percival yanked it open.

Though Gary reached out to stop Percival from doing something stupid, it wasn't needed.

Percival halted at the sight of the open door. His head cocked, fury replaced by confusion. "Harold?"

Gary stiffened beside him, and together they both ducked and leaned partially in. "Oh, goodness. Harold!"

Percival reared back, searched the crowd, and his gaze landed on my mom. "Phyllis, call an ambulance. He's hurt. I think Harold is hurt bad."

I glanced in, managing to see between Gary and Percival's arms as they unbuckled seat belts. Percival started to move the body, but Gary stopped him. "We should wait. We might do more damage."

An older man sat behind the wheel, two frail arms lying like dead weight in his lap. His entire body twitched, and his eyes, so wide, stared straight ahead, though didn't seem to be seeing. Cuts from the glass freckled his face.

Percival laid a gentle hand on Harold's shoulder. "It's okay, buddy. Help's on the way. It's going to be okay."

It wasn't until that moment that it clicked who Harold was. I'd only seen him once. And now, with him bloody and shaken, he seemed even more ancient and frail. Carla's grandfather.

It was only a matter of minutes before the ambulance arrived, as well as the police. Susan cast an accusatory glare my direction but didn't comment. She'd been the first on scene and moved away to make room for the paramedics. She was taking Percival's and Gary's statements.

"He just ran his car into the shop?" Branson, who'd arrived a few minutes after Susan, looked back and forth between the car, the gaping hole in the building, the huddled masses of the other adult members of my family, and me. "Everyone else was inside, and they're really okay?"

"They were all toward the back of the store. Miraculously." I shuddered, the vision of how differently this might have gone if one or more of them had been near the front. I shoved the thought aside. "We were..." I swallowed, my mouth dry. "We were supposed to begin clearing out the space today to start getting it ready for Zelda and Verona's shop."

"You all are lucky. Very." His green eyes narrowed and flashed up at me. "Watson? Is he okay?"

My heart warmed at his concern, and I gave my first smile. "Yes. He's safe. He's in the Cozy Corgi with Katie and Leo. They took him and my nephews and nieces inside."

"Thank goodness." He gave my hand a quick squeeze and inspected the scene once more. "This could've been so much worse. So, so much worse. With all the tourists, Harold cutting across traffic, you and your family."

We fell silent as the paramedics transferred Harold from the car to a stretcher. He was still trembling, eyes still impossibly wide, but he was mumbling incoherently.

"Grandpa!" At that moment, Carla burst through the tape that had been keeping the crowds roped off several yards away. Her eyes were frantic as she searched the scene. She'd probably just heard and ran from Black Bear Roaster. Although maybe she'd been at home, as it had taken her several minutes to get here. Not that it mattered. She spotted Harold on the stretcher and sprinted toward him, crying.

Branson left my side, rushing toward her, but Susan stepped away from Percival and Gary and got to her first, wrapping her arms around Carla in a combination restraint and embrace, stopping her before she crashed into the stretcher. "He's fine. Carla, he's alive.

Carla struggled for a second, still reaching for him but then gave in to Susan's embrace. "He's not supposed to drive. I didn't know he took the keys. I have no idea what he was doing. He's not supposed to drive."

Susan stroked Carla's hair, a loving gesture I never would've pictured Susan capable of making. "He'll be fine. Going to give him all the help he needs."

"I hadn't even realized he'd left. Had no idea he took my car." She let out a ragged cry and caught her breath, or at least attempted to. "He's shaking. Look at him. He won't stop shaking."

She tried to break free from Susan's strong arms once more. But Susan held tight. "It's just shock. Doesn't mean anything. It's just shock."

"No!" Carla shook her head, blonde hair flying. "He has seizures. He's having a seizure." She glanced around as if searching. "My purse. Where's my purse? I have his medication in my purse."

Seizures.

That frozen moment before the impact flitted through my mind, frozen in clarity. Right before I fell over Watson. Harold's wide and glassy eyes behind the windshield as he careened toward us. Seizures. *That's* what I had seen. Maybe he hadn't even been aware of what was happening, or if so, couldn't do anything about it.

I hoped it was the first. I couldn't imagine how terrifying it would've been if he'd been aware that he was about to crash into people, into a building, and couldn't stop it.

Branson's words came back to me. It could've been so, so much worse.

Carla was slipping into hysterics, not that I could blame her, for once. She demanded Susan help her find her purse to get her grandfather's medication.

The paramedics were already loading Harold into the back of the ambulance.

In her terror and panic, Carla continued to look around as if someone was holding her purse intentionally just out of reach.

Her wild green gaze latched on to me. She froze and then rushed forward, breaking free of Susan's hold.

"You!" She shoved a finger my way as she rocketed toward me. "This is your fault. He's been a complete mess the past couple of days knowing that you're asking questions. Trying to pin this on me!"

Though a second late, Susan rushed after Carla,

but Branson stepped between us stopping Carla's trajectory a heartbeat before she made contact. "Calm down, Carla. Get ahold of yourself." His tone held none of the care and concern Susan had displayed.

"It's your fault." Carla continued to try to get at me, attempting to crawl over Branson in her fury. "Do you know what stress you put him under? Put us all under? He knows you've been targeting me since you moved into town. Everyone knows."

"Knock it off, Carla. Or you'll be taking a time-out in the back of a cop car." Branson angled her away, but despite his strength, nearly lost his grip in the face of her rage.

"Shut up, Wexler," Susan growled at Branson even as she slipped her arm over Carla, helping him hold her back. "You're making things worse."

"Come on, darling." Mom's small hand touched my back and then nudged me to move. "Let's go in your shop. We'll give them some space."

Though it was hard to turn away from Carla, I looked down at my tiny mother, who was calm, strong, and grounded. I nodded.

"That's it. Good girl. Good girl." Mom patted my back as we walked toward the front door of the bookshop. "We'll hang out there till they're ready for us.

We'll have some of Katie's scones, and she'll make you one of those dirty chai you like so much." She paused, considering. "Or maybe something more soothing. A nice decaffeinated Earl Grey or something. That might be a better choice."

As we walked through the door, Watson crashed into me again, and I sank to the floor so he could assure himself I was fine once more.

EIGHT

Aspen Grove's ability to blend in with the side of the mountain was rather astonishing considering it was a sprawling stucco structure. It was a combination of Santa Fe and old-time mountain style. Kind of charming, really.

I paused at the oversized wooden doors and glanced toward Barry. "You sure this is a good idea? What if Carla shows up? She was ready to skin me alive yesterday."

"Nah, you're fine." He waved me off. "Plus, we called the coffee shop; Carla answered the phone. We won't be here that long." Barry held the door open for me, his blue-and-green tie-dyed tank top and lavender yoga pants looking even more outlandish than usual next to the formal ambience.

My nerves surprised me. We were going to visit a sick old man who'd had a car crash the day before. We weren't doing anything wrong. And even if

Carla did show up, she'd had a day to calm down. Right... as if Carla's temper cooled in merely a day.

We walked to the front desk where a larger woman sat behind a computer screen, though her gaze was fixed on the soap opera playing in the spacious common room across from her.

"Martha!" Barry slapped his hands down on the edge of the front desk in way of greeting.

The poor woman nearly fell out of her seat, and clutched at her chest as she sucked in a breath. Her widened eyes narrowed as she whipped toward my stepfather and looked up and down his outfit. "Barry Adams." Her tone left no mystery to how she felt about his arrival. Barry was most definitely an acquired taste.

"Martha *Booger*." He beamed, and knowing Barry, either wasn't aware of the reaction he stirred in Martha or simply didn't care. "Goodness, we're being formal today."

Her attention flicked back to the soap opera, then returned to Barry, and finally to me, giving me the once-over as well. Her stare held when they reached my mustard-yellow boots poking out from my sage-green skirt.

It seemed she found me to be an acquired taste as well. Good thing I'd left Watson at home.

Although, she seemed as grumpy as my little corgi, so maybe it would've been kismet.

Doubtful.

"We're here to see Harold White." Barry smacked the desk again in declaration, once more causing Martha to flinch, then reached for the guest-sign-in book and scrawled his name before sliding it to me.

"I don't remember getting a call from you this morning, Mr. Adams. We've talked about this before." Martha's lips narrowed as her nose crinkled.

"And even more formal, *Ms.* Booger." Barry chuckled. "And I told *you* before, I'm a free spirit, never know what I'll do one minute to the next. I can hardly make plans this morning for something I might do later in the day."

"It's not even noon yet, Mr. Adams."

Barry lifted the plate Mom had sent with us from my hands and peeled back the plastic wrap. "Here, have a cinnamon roll for your troubles. My wife sent them along for Harold, but I'm sure he won't mind if you have one."

For a moment, it looked like Martha was going to stay strong, but then she reached toward the plate, picked off the largest one, and plopped back in the chair. "Move it along, Barry. You're blocking the television."

He obliged, grabbing my hand and pulling me with him before I could sign the logbook as he waved over his shoulder. "Always a pleasure, Martha."

We were partially down the hallway when I dared whisper to him, "Is her last name actually Booger, or do you just call her that because she doesn't like you?"

He halted and turned to me, brows creased. "What do you mean she doesn't like me?"

I couldn't think of what to say to that.

Not that it mattered. Barry glanced back at Martha, considered, and then shook his head. "That's just Martha's way. She's a doll. We see each other a few times a week. You get to be my age and most of your friends end up in a place like this. Almost like a fraternity." He scowled. "Not that I was ever in one of those capitalist, misogynistic, drone factories."

"I'm sure you're right." Knowing Barry, I could sense we were on the verge of a political rant. Wealthy or not, Barry Adams remained the hippie-dippie, combination of flower child and mountain man he'd always been. "But didn't we need to get Harold's room number?"

"Weren't you listening, Fred? I'm here all the time. And Harold is one of the gang." He wobbled his head back and forth as if judging the veracity of his claim. "Well, kinda. He was a few years older than us growing up, but he married Dolana, and she was definitely part of our gang, Lord rest her soul." He slipped his hand into mine again and led me down the hall. "Now remember, I know you're hoping to get some details about what he might've noticed the other day at the coffee shop, but our priority is to visit a friend who's clearly having a rough time. I didn't know the seizures had gotten so bad."

I allowed him to lead me on, and for a moment, marveled at the feel of his hand in mine. In the months I had been in Estes, we'd gone from a caring yet rather awkward relationship to him acquiring the semblance of a father role. Though he could never replace what my dad meant to me, nor would he try, which made all the difference.

Barry gave the briefest of knocks on a partially open door, then walked through like he owned the place.

The room was small but cozy and clean. Harold White was asleep in a twin bed against the wall. Though there were railings attached, it was clear they'd attempted to stay away from the typical hospital bed feel.

He'd appeared so small and out of place behind the counter of Black Bear Roaster, with his too large, too white dentures beaming at me. But lying there asleep, bandages scattered over his face covering the cuts from the shattered windshield, he looked even smaller, and so frail. I couldn't blame Carla for being protective of him. If he truly had been stressed about me asking questions regarding his granddaughter, there might be actual reason to be concerned. He didn't seem like he could handle too much stress.

I motioned to the door. "We should let him rest."

Barry studied him, sadness flicking over his face. "Let's give it a minute. He might wake up." He slid the plate of cinnamon rolls Mom had sent onto the bedside table before taking a seat in the closest chair and placing his hand over Harold's.

Something about the gesture caused my throat to constrict, and I turned away, focusing on the large picture window on the opposite wall. I blinked away the hint of tears and then sucked in a breath and stepped toward the window seat. "Oh my goodness."

We'd driven just a little bit out of town to get to Aspen Grove, but I hadn't noticed how far up the sides of the mountain we'd gone. In front of us lay the entire Estes Park valley, looking like a charming toy village nestled in the embrace of mountains. Elkhorn Avenue was easily visible running through downtown and then carving its way into the national park. With the smattering of clouds casting lazy shadows, it easily could have belonged on a postcard.

I really did love living there. "What a spectacular view."

"The view is nice, but you get your own tiny little apartment if you spring for The Spruce." The gravelly voice was strained and quiet.

I turned to find Harold looking at me.

"The Spruce costs about five times as much, though."

"Yeah..." Barry moved closer, pulling Harold's attention away from me. "But the nurses here sure are prettier."

Harold managed to laugh but winced at the effort. "True, but nobody is as pretty as my Dolana."

"Well, of course not, Harold. Can't get prettier than that angel." Barry sighed heavily, then broke the moment by motioning to me and then the plate of cinnamon rolls. "Fred and I thought we'd drop by, and Phyllis made you some goodies that surely aren't on the diet this place has you on. She sends her love. She had some appointments planned this morning already, but she's gonna pop in tomorrow sometime to see you."

"That'd be nice." Harold blinked slowly and looked back at me, his eyes hardening slightly. "Carla didn't hurt Eustace. And if you're here to try to get me to say otherwise, you might as well get going."

"I'm not, Mr. White. I'm sorry you're worried about that. I don't think Carla would try to kill anybody." I was nearly certain I believed that. "We just wanted to check on you." That part wasn't true, at least not completely. Barry was right; I was hoping to uncover a lead. Even if Carla wasn't involved, maybe Harold had seen something that day, knew who plated the scone for Eustace. "You gave us quite a scare yesterday."

He attempted to sit up a little straighter, winced again, and relaxed back into the pillow. "Nobody's hurt, right? Carla said nobody was hurt." He sounded frantic, desperate.

"No, Harold. Everybody's okay." Barry brightened, and it showed how much more I knew him that I could tell some of it was forced, for once. "Truth be told, you did us a favor. My girls are wanting to revamp that shop anyway. You saved us some time."

Harold studied me for a few more moments, then refocused on Barry and grinned. "I do what I can.

Can't say I remember helping you out, but I'll be happy to charge. Maybe enough to get a month stay at The Spruce."

"There you go again, trying to leave all these pretty nurses behind." Even Barry's naturally cheerful nature couldn't hide his concern. "The seizures are that bad? You really don't remember?"

He shook his head. "Sure don't."

"And what in the green blazes were you doing driving, young man?" Wasn't sure I'd ever heard Barry sound so authoritarian before.

"Don't you start too. Carla was in here ranting and raving, soon as I got back from the hospital yesterday evening. Accused me of stealing her car. Told me I'll never find the keys with how good she's gonna hide them from now on." He seemed to deflate and grow even smaller. "Hardly feel like a man anymore. No freedom at all. Stuck in here. Can't drive, working in the coffee shop all day. At least at The Spruce, you can pretend like you've got your own place."

Barry pointed at the window. "You don't get this view with The Spruce, Harold. That's gotta be worth something."

Harold simply shook his head. "Seen it all my life, Barry. Maybe it looks different to you now, seeing as you own quite a bit of it. None of its mine." He turned away, staring at the wall. "It's just a view of other people's stuff."

I glanced out the window again and struggled to picture the stunning expanse the way Harold saw it. I couldn't. I couldn't find anything depressing or hopeless there. It was beautiful, wild and free. Full of hope and possibility.

Then again, I wasn't a fragile old man lying in a tiny twin bed who had his life dictated by nurses and his granddaughter.

Suddenly, I knew I couldn't ask Harold any more questions about that day in the coffee shop. He was going through enough. And anything he said would be slanted from his dim view of the world.

Leaving the window, I squeezed Barry on the shoulder as I walked by. "I'm going to let you gentlemen have your space and privacy. I don't want to intrude." I started to pat Harold's quilt-covered legs, then thought better of it and waved instead. "It's good to see you, Mr. White. I hope you're feeling better soon and that you're back at the coffee shop before too long."

He didn't respond.

I caught Barry's attention as I walked out the

door. "I'll meet you up front whenever you're ready. Take your time."

He smiled in way of acknowledgment and turned back to his friend.

Heaviness settled over me as I headed toward the reception area. Aspen Grove had seemed beautiful and charming, but now it all seemed rather depressing.

Just as I neared reception, barking filled the hall- way, and I glanced up in the nick of time to see two half-crazed corgis rocketing toward me, tongues lolling and eyes frantic with excitement. As one, the pair launched themselves airborne when they were less than two feet from me, crashed into my shins, and for the second time in two days, I hit the floor while covered in a tumble of fur and corgi kisses.

NINE

"My goodness, they just adore you." Paulie Mertz stood above me, hands on his hips, a pleased smile on his thin, asymmetrical face. "That, and I'm sure they smell Watson." He tore his pleased gaze from the corgi attack and searched the hallway, including the direction he'd traveled. "Where is that little guy? He should join the fun."

"Paulie." I managed to get ahold of the tricolored corgi's collar and pulled him away slightly. Not much, as corgis are strong both in body and willpower, but enough that I thought I could avoid another french kiss. I wasn't so lucky with the red one and got a mouthful of nose before I could close it in time. Jerking my head away, I tried again. "Paulie, can you please get Flotsam off me? I think I've got Jetsam under control."

"Of course, of course!" Paulie bent down and grabbed the leash of the tricolor, and pulled him away, forcing me to release my grip on his collar. The red one took advantage of the opportunity and gave me an earful of tongue.

With a shudder, I transferred my hold onto his collar, found the leash, and thrust it in Paulie's direction. "This one. I meant this one."

"Oh! Sorry. But he's Jetsam." Paulie grabbed the red corgi's leash and took a few steps back, pulling both dogs with him, though each of them was straining to get to me once more.

Barely managing to refrain from commenting about not caring which one was which, only that they keep their distance, I pushed myself to my knees, used my sleeves to wipe the copious amounts of drool off my face and then stood, placing my hand on the wall for support. "Thank you. That was... intense."

And still Paulie beamed. "Yep, they just love coming here. They get so much attention."

"Oh? Do you have family here or something?" I slipped my hand into one of my sleeves and used the fabric over my finger to get the moisture out of my ear, at least as much as I could.

Paulie's expression fell. "No. No family in town, remember?"

Despite my irritation, I felt a pang of guilt at my

thoughtlessness. Paulie had mentioned he was alone in town and made it abundantly clear that he was lonely and desperate for friendship. I'd promised myself I was going to do a better job of making him feel welcome; I hadn't followed through on that. "I do recall. Sorry, Paulie. I wasn't thinking."

"No problem." His smile was back. Though less frantic, he was nearly as friendly as his two crazy corgis. The tricolor, Jetsam... no, Flotsam... lunged at me again, his tongue long enough he nearly made contact with my boots. Paulie readjusted his stance.

I took a step back. "Who are you here visiting? Mr. White?"

He puzzled for a second, and then his eyes cleared. "Carla's grandfather, right." Paulie shook his head. "No, the boys and I come here at least once a week. My way of giving back to the community. They make the retirees happy. For a lot of them, it's the highlight of their week." Another headshake, though this one slower. "But we steer clear of Mr. White's room. He's kinda like Carla. They aren't very dog friendly."

It didn't seem to me that a person's aversion to Flotsam and Jetsam indicated any level of not being dog friendly, but I kept the opinion to myself. "It's nice of you to try to make people's days better, Paulie."

He shrugged and again his cheerfulness faded, but just for a second. "It's good for me too. Estes is beautiful, but it can be a little isolating."

More guilt. Maybe it was too little too late, but I might as well try. "Barry is going to be visiting with Harold for a while I would imagine. I was just on my way to the reception area. Want to join?"

"Seriously?"

The hope and excitement in his tone only added to my determination to do a better job of reaching out. "Of course, if you have time. I don't want to interrupt anything."

"You're not!" He glanced toward the reception desk, then lowered his voice. "But do you mind if we maybe chat outside? Ms. Booger doesn't like the boys... or me, all that much."

I matched his whispered tone. "That's probably a good idea. I got the impression she's not overly fond of Barry or me either."

"Well, that's strange, I can't imagine anyone not simply adoring you." He thrust one of the leashes into my hand. "Here. Take Jetsam. Watson isn't around here anywhere?"

"No. He's a little grumpier than your two, if you

remember." The instant I took Jetsam's leash, he began jumping all over me, and somehow managed to get his head under my skirt and started lathering my shins with his tongue. I was going to have to shower before heading back into the bookshop. I nudged him with my boot, but it was pointless. "Watson would probably just sit in the corner if we came here to visit everyone. Unless they had snacks."

It was the wrong word to use—both Flotsam and Jetsam went into hysterics.

The corgis forgot about me, thankfully, within a few minutes of going outside. We found a wrought-iron-and-wood bench at a little seating area close to the front door, and Paulie tied their leashes to a tree, allowing them to get lost in their exploration of smells and destruction of pinecones.

"Are you here investigating? I've heard you're on the case?" Paulie turned his back on the corgis and swiveled toward me. Hands folded in his lap, his brown eyes sparkled in excitement. "Were you interviewing Carla's grandfather?"

I'd wondered at Carla's anger at me the day before, saying that Harold's seizures were worse due to the stress over me looking into Eustace's death and fear that I was trying to pin it all on Carla. And yet, here we were again. "You heard I was on a case?" I shook my head, feeling ridiculous as I heard my own words. "Not that I could ever be on the case. I sell books, remember, I'm not a police officer or detective."

"Right." He tapped his temple and gave a conspiratorial wink. "You just sell books. And Diana Prince was just a nurse."

I nearly laughed at the comparison, but despite myself couldn't help but feel flattered, though I quickly sidestepped. "Besides, the official word is that Eustace choked. What is there to ask questions about?"

"Really?" He cocked his head. "You believe that?"

"Don't you?" Maybe Paulie did know something. Just my luck that the one person who might agree with me about Eustace being a victim of murder would be Paulie Mertz.

"I hadn't thought about it until I heard you were on the case." He shrugged. "But it makes sense. He was horrible to me when I was setting up the pet shop. He's horrible to almost everybody." He flinched. "I wasn't saying that I killed him. Or that he deserved to be murdered just because he was horrible to me."

"I know that, Paulie. I wasn't thinking you tried to kill him or anyone else." I patted his knee, then drew my hand back quickly lest I gave the wrong idea. "But why do you keep saying that I'm on the case if you didn't think about someone trying to kill him? Who did you hear it from?"

"Roxanne mentioned it last night during our meeting of the Feathered Friends Brigade." He glanced over his shoulder when Flotsam and Jetsam started barking at a ground squirrel, then looked back at me after the little rodent escaped. "You're quite the hero there, you know. Even if Petra did get in trouble for having that bird. Myrtle thinks you hung the moon."

I had a feeling not everyone in the bird club would agree with Myrtle's estimation of me. And given her initial distance, I doubted Myrtle herself felt that way about me all the time. And I hadn't seen Roxanne in months. People must've really been talking for her to be part of the gossip. Before I could think of an appropriate response, Paulie continued.

"Plus, Athena said you came to see her. She could tell you were on the trail of somebody."

I'd forgotten about Paulie and Athena being

friends, despite sitting with them at the espresso party the other day. They were such an odd couple. Although, for Paulie, that sort of made sense. Still, with as classy and refined as Athena seemed, I couldn't imagine her tolerating Flotsam and Jetsam for very long. Or little Pearl coping with the two of them, for that matter. "Athena didn't have any kind words to say about Eustace Beaker, that's for sure."

"Oh, no. She hated that man." Paulie's eyes widened as he shook his head emphatically. "He was horrible to her. I mean, I know he was horrible to a lot of people, but he was *really* horrible to her."

Unable to stop myself, I leaned forward, interest piqued. "He was? *Worse* to Athena than most people?"

He nodded. "I can't say worse than most people, but bad enough. Worse than he was to me, anyway. He just tried to keep me from opening a business. He tried to ruin Athena's whole life, at least from what she says."

I was surprised he was being so transparent, surely he knew how he was making it sound. Although, Paulie didn't seem that relationally astute. And he was desperate enough for friendship that he'd probably say anything that crossed his mind to keep the conversation going. The realization caused my guilt to fester once more, but I couldn't hold myself back. "What did he do?"

"He was awful. Well, this happened before I moved here. A long time ago actually, but I can totally see him doing it."

Feeling like a completely manipulative and awful person, I reached forward and touched Paulie's knee lightly and repeated my question. "What did he do?"

"Athena didn't always write obituaries for the paper, you know. She had a..." Paulie's expression changed, and he leaned back as he abruptly quit speaking. He blinked, and for the first time it seemed he was studying me, judging for himself what he thought of Winifred Page instead of only seeing her as a potential friend in his lonely life. "Athena wouldn't hurt Mr. Beaker. She wouldn't hurt anybody."

I considered sugarcoating or backpedaling. But the idea of either left a bitter taste in my mouth, and Paulie had been nothing but kind to me since I'd moved to Estes and attempted friendship on repeated occasions. I owed him better than trying to manipulate him. "Like we've already said, Paulie, as far as the police are concerned, Mr. Beaker simply choked on a scone and died. They don't expect foul play."

"But *you* do."

And again, he was more attuned than I gave him credit for. "I do. Though I have absolutely no shred of proof or reason to believe that, other than my own gut feeling."

Again, he studied me. There were shadows in his eyes, different than before. The darkness told me there was more to Paulie than simply feeling like an outcast. He had seen things. "That's more than enough reason for me to believe somebody killed him, if your gut tells you that."

It didn't feel like flattery, just a calm statement of belief. One I didn't think I deserved, especially from him. "Maybe. Maybe not."

"If you think he was killed, then he was." It seemed Paulie had decided. He sat up straighter, and his tone hardened. "Athena wouldn't hurt anybody, Fred. Your gut might tell you that someone killed Mr. Beaker, but mine tells me that Athena is good. She's the closest friend I have in town."

Fair enough. "I'm glad you have her. And she seems very nice." This time when I reached forward and patted Paulie's knee, there was nothing manipulative or forced about it. "To be honest, I found her rather charming, smart, and a little intimidating."

He chuckled and offered a soft smile. "So, kind of like you."

That took me back for a second. I couldn't imagine anyone finding me intimidating. Well, that wasn't true. There were plenty of men who were intimidated by any tall woman who was willing to speak her mind, but other than that, I didn't see that as one of my qualities.

Thankfully, I didn't have to figure out how to respond. With a decisive nod, Paulie began again. "I suppose there's no reason not to tell you the story. I don't really think it's a secret. And even if it was, I think you'll find it out anyway now that you think there's a reason to look into Athena."

"Paulie, she's your friend. You don't owe me any explanation at all. I'm not the police, remember? I just sell books, and if you ask Officer Green, she'll tell you that all I do is snoop and stick my nose in places it doesn't belong."

"Officer Green." He rolled his eyes. "She doesn't care for me either. Of course, neither does Sergeant Wexler, but you two get along well, so maybe he's not as bad as he seems."

It wasn't the first time he referenced Branson in

an unflattering light. Though, in regard to Paulie, I figured I could easily be painted with the same brush. "Either way, I'm sorry you felt I was pressuring you to break a friend's confidence."

"Athena had several jobs at the paper years ago." Paulie launched in, ignoring the out I'd offered. "She reviewed the restaurants in town, school plays, stuff like that. She was even the senior editor for the entertainment and social articles. When Black Bear Roaster opened, she wrote a review. An honest review, so it talked about how the food wasn't very good and how the service was somewhat lacking in warmth." He smiled mischievously, and I was a little surprised to find that my fondness for the man was growing once more. "Mr. Beaker went on a tirade, fired her from the paper—he's one of the owners of *The Chipmunk Chronicles*, you know. To me it seems kind of silly. He clearly can't stand Carla, but Athena said he took it as a personal insult. Nearly broke Athena's heart. She said those were the happiest years of her life in that position. She loved it."

No wonder she hated the man. "You said she was fired. She writes the obituaries now."

"Yeah." He nodded. "But Gerald Jackson also has a large holding in the newspaper. He and Athena are friends. He pulled some weight and got her job back. Not the one she had or wanted, but still."

"Did you say Gerald Jackson?" Maybe I still had corgi slobber in my ears. Gerald was friends with Barry, Percival, and Gary, and was a lawyer, but I'd been thoroughly unimpressed every time I met the man. "He stood up to Mr. Beaker and got Athena her job back?"

"He sure did." Paulie checked on the dogs once more before turning back to me, his expression serious. "We're friends, Fred, so I'm going to be up front. I'm going to tell Athena that I told you the story. I don't want either one of you thinking I'd lie to my friends."

I most definitely did not deserve Paulie labeling me as a friend, but I was determined to change that. "I admire that quality, Paulie."

His story about Athena made sense. I could easily see Eustace acting in such a way. I couldn't blame Athena for feeling how she did if the man had stolen her dream in such an abrupt and unfair manner. Although...

"If Athena has that history with the Beaker family, why in the world would she attend Carla's espresso launch?"

Paulie laughed and nearly glowed with pride.

"That's Athena for you. Nobody tells her where she can or can't go. And she doesn't take flak from anybody. She goes into Black Bear Roaster at least once a week, sometimes with her computer to write the obituaries, just to rub it in Carla's and Mr. Beaker's faces."

I barely knew the woman, but I could see her doing that.

But maybe Paulie was blinded by friendship in this case. Maybe rubbing their noses in it with her presence wasn't revenge enough. And there wouldn't be a more public payback than what had happened, and she'd had front row seats to the show.

Paulie clucked his tongue, pulling me back to the moment. "I can tell what you're thinking, Fred. She didn't do it. Athena would never do anything like that."

There was no reason to deny my thoughts. "Like I said, Paulie, I'm not the police. I just poke around. And if Athena is the kind of woman you say she is, then me poking around won't change that fact, will it?"

"That's true, I suppose."

Some of his insecurity came back into his tone. "I'm still going to tell her what I've said. I hope that doesn't make you mad at me."

"Hey, you two! Or should I say four!" Barry's voice called out, and I turned to see him walking toward us. I gave a little wave before turning back to Paulie.

"It most definitely doesn't make me mad. If anything, I respect you for it. You being an honorable person definitely will not hurt our friendship, Paulie." I smiled in a way I hoped showed my genuine growing affection for him.

"Thanks." His voice was thick, and he sniffed.

And then Barry was upon us. Flotsam and Jetsam went wild. Granted, it seemed they went into excited conniption fits over lint, but still, my stepfather proved, in at least three out of three cases, to be the equivalent of catnip for corgis.

Seeing the gaping hole in the wall of Sinful Bites only increased my feeling of guilt when Watson and I arrived back at the Cozy Corgi. Thick, opaque plastic had been secured, blocking the view inside of the shop, and yellow caution tape formed a large X, making it clear the area wasn't safe.

Maybe *I* needed to come with caution tape.

Harold White refused to leave my mind on the way back into town from Aspen Grove. He'd been so depressed, and I couldn't say I blamed him. Beautiful view or not, I couldn't imagine having to spend my life stuck between that tiny room and Carla's coffee shop. And then, to make matters worse for him, though I didn't think I'd done anything to prompt it, the poor old man was worried I was trying to get his granddaughter charged with murder.

I hadn't gone around town asking endless questions, though I'd been planning on doing that very thing. Even so, it seemed everyone assumed I was going to take it upon myself to prove that Eustace Beaker was murdered and then point out who that particular murderer was.

Was I that predictable?

Apparently.

Watson pulled on his leash, urging me to quit standing on the sidewalk and go into the bookshop, but I couldn't tear myself away from staring at the caution tape.

Had I caused that? By doing what Susan Green constantly accused me of—poking my nose where it didn't belong? Had I stressed out an old man so much that it exacerbated his seizures and nearly cost my uncles their lives in the process?

On some level, I knew that was ridiculous. It was. I hadn't accused Carla of anything, and the only questioning I'd done had been with Athena. Granted, I'd gone to the assisted-living home that morning with the intention of seeing what I could uncover from Harold, but still. I hadn't caused this.

Though, somewhere inside me, a little voice whispered that maybe I had.

Talk about a morning full of looking in the mirror and not loving what I saw. First Harold, then Paulie. Gracious as Paulie was, I'd been nearly as guilty as the rest of the town of leaving him alienated and alone.

That was what I needed to focus on. Quit worrying about trying to solve a murder—more accurately, quit enjoying the sensation of solving them before the police—and focus on simply doing what I'd come here to do. Sell books and build a life that was comfortable and that I could be proud of. I needed to pay attention to good people who wanted to be my friend instead of looking for poison when someone choked.

Watson whimpered and finally managed to pull my attention away from the hole in the wall.

I met his pleading brown gaze and made him a promise. "All right. We'll go in. From now on, you'll be able to spend as much time as you want sleeping in the sunshine by the windows. I'll quit dragging you all around town like you're the George to my Nancy or the Lacey to my Cagney." I ruffled the fur on the top of his head. "Or the Watson to my Holmes, for that matter. You can just be Watson— furry best friend and bottomless treat disposal."

His fox ears pointed straight up in the air, his eyes brightened, and he gave a bunny hop.

With that he made my heart soften and managed to help me laugh. "I said the word, didn't I? Well, come on, then. Let's go see Katie and get you your favorite treat."

The rest of the morning was spent making good on my promise. I had just enough time to get Watson his treats, and a dirty chai and chocolate chip scone for myself after a quick greeting with Katie, and then I was lost to the world of retail. Beautiful, beautiful book retail.

A hipster couple visiting from Portland wanted a field guide containing an exhaustive list of safe edible fungi native to Rocky Mountain National Park. I had yet to quit being surprised how many copies of that book I sold.

A woman who appeared to be in her early twenties, with so many facial piercings that I kept losing count as she spoke, found the perfect cozy mystery based on my suggestion. Though, that one took me a while. I'd assumed she was looking for the darker, supernatural variety of that genre. Instead, she was drawn to a series about an eighty-year-old church secretary who solved murders from her Meals on Wheels van.

Half an hour later, an elderly lady who appeared to be the embodiment of the Meals on Wheels sleuth herself, surprised me by asking for the steamiest romance novel I had in stock, but one with a nondescript cover and title so the other members of the church choir wouldn't suspect.

To my surprise, Myrtle Bantam came in around lunchtime and didn't ask for books about birds, and proved Paulie's claim of her feelings about me were accurate when she bought a vibrant yellow hoodie with a large emblem of the Cozy Corgi logo emblazoned on the front.

That interaction alleviated my guilt somewhat. At least my snooping had made *Myrtle's* life better.

By the time midafternoon rolled around, there'd been barely enough time to run back up to the bakery and get a snack and a second dirty chai. Katie and I shared quick smiles but little else as she was slammed as well, even more than me.

This was the life I'd envisioned. My own little world, my own little bookshop. *Better* than I'd envisioned, with the soothing sounds and comforting aromas from the bakery upstairs filling my space. An endless string of patrons falling in love with the Cozy Corgi and needing my help to discover their next great escape. And in a couple more weeks, if what the locals said was true, the real wave of tourists would arrive and then I'd really be swept away.

And through it all, Watson lay by the front windows in his typical spot, surrounded by the general-fiction and new-release section—snoozing, snoring, and stretching contentedly, only shifting slightly to keep his napping place firmly centered in the sunlight.

I was so caught up in helping customers and willfully devoting myself to this, and *only* this, aspect of my life that it took me a second to recognize the boy when he came in. I was halfway through my greeting when I did a double take and realized who I was speaking to. And once more, guilt filtered back in. This time, I didn't have to seek his name.

"Nick. Hi. What can I do for you?" I was certain the teenage barista from Black Bear Roaster had never been in before. Maybe Carla had sent him down to spy on me to see if I was snooping, giving her grandfather more reasons to be stressed out and sick. Or maybe to serve me with papers because she was going to sue me for damages to her car.

Could that even be a thing?

The speculations tumbled so fast that I barely caught Nick's first words as he shook his head. "I'm not Nick. I'm Ben." He pointed to his bottom lip. "I have a scar here on the left. Nick has a scar on his right eyebrow." He then tapped his head, his voice so quiet that it was barely audible over the soft piped-in music and background noise from the bakery. "And my hair's a little longer."

I stared at the barista, trying to make sense of his words. As I was doing so, Watson pattered over and nudged the boy's shin with his forehead.

The kid startled, looked down, then smiled, seeming to relax for the first time as he bent and stroked Watson's back.

I marveled at the two of them. Well, really I marveled at Watson. I had yet to figure out what made him attracted to someone. He wasn't a people person, or a people pup rather. He tolerated them if he had to or they were offering him treats, but every once in a while, there was one he seemed to want to know. Or, in the case of Leo and Barry, worship.

The barista folded his lanky body as he crouched to really give Watson affection, and he smiled up at me. His dark eyes were shadowed, maybe a little pained, but he brightened in Watson's presence. "I like your dog."

"His name is Watson, and he likes you. That's pretty rare, Nick." At the crease that formed between the boy's brows, I realized my mistake and had to think back for a second to recall his name. "Sorry, Ben, right?"

He nodded. "Yeah, scar on my lip and longer hair, remember?"

There was only one explanation, the obvious one. "You must be Nick's twin brother. I didn't even know he was a twin." What a stupid thing to say. Up until a hot second ago, I hadn't even bothered to know the barista's name, let alone inquire about his familial situation.

"Yep." Again, he was barely audible as he nodded, and then Ben refocused on Watson, and I swore the two of them gazed into each other's eyes and had some sort of conversation. Then, to my utter shock, he pressed his forehead to Watson's, gave a final pat, and stood.

Not only had Watson allowed it to happen, but he continued to sit, comfortably, at Ben's feet, not even begging for a snack or demanding more attention.

I was completely thrown off and bewildered. Finally, I refocused on Ben, who was watching me expectantly. His gaze was so intense that it was slightly uncomfortable, like maybe he could see the guilt I'd been battling with that morning. Although if he could, he didn't seem to be condemning me for it.

Good grief, what was my problem?

Demanding my brain to think sensibly, I gave

him my best shopkeeper smile. "Well, Ben, what can I do for you? You searching for a particular book?"

He shook his head, opened his mouth, then closed it again. After a second his tongue darted out and licked his lips. Poor kid was nervous, which in turn, made me nervous once more.

Watson scooted a little closer, resting his flank against Ben's leg.

It was all the encouragement he needed. His dark brown eyes lasered directly into mine, and though his voice wavered, his gaze didn't. "My folks said I either need to apply to colleges or get a job. Don't really want to do either. I want to write books. But... in the meantime... I figure working at a bookstore would be second best."

Once more I felt a little slow on the uptake. "Katie and I"—I pointed upstairs as if he couldn't figure it out—"are doing interviews for the bakery. Is that what you are thinking?"

He grimaced. "No. I didn't know about that. But I'm more curious about the bookshop. I don't like to cook. That's Nick's thing, not mine."

We'd planned on getting the bakery squared away first. Interviewing employees for the bakery and the bookshop at the same time seemed like too much, but when I envisioned who I wanted to work here, it most definitely hadn't been a kid who was barely loud enough to be heard over soft jazz.

No big deal. It would be easy enough, just tell him I wasn't hiring quite yet. But let him know he could interview later.

Watson shifted again and chuffed, bringing my attention to him as if he could read my mind.

Maybe he could.

In that moment I was certain I could read his.

How strange. Although, not really. For his grumpy disposition and seemingly only caring about snacks and naps, Watson occasionally displayed nearly mystical awareness of someone's pain and need. That was how he came into my life, after all. Wandered up to me at my darkest, lowest moment, then changed my world.

I looked at the barista's twin once more. "How old are you, Ben?"

"Eighteen." He cleared his throat. "I graduate high school in two weeks. But for this last semester, I only go half days anyway. I could work afternoons as soon as tomorrow if you want."

A million questions flitted through my mind. Did his parents know he was applying here? What about his brother? Did Carla know?

That last one gave me pause. There was so much

conflict between the two of us. Surely having her barista's brother work for me would somehow be twisted into me sinking my claws into her in some new way.

But that wasn't Ben's fault. And the kid was eighteen. Well... that wasn't right either. If he was eighteen, he wasn't a kid.

"What kind of books do you want to write?"

His eyes widened, and though his volume got no louder, his passion was clearly evident in his words. "I've been mapping out a series for years. About a detective named Coyote." He hesitated, but just for a second. "In my culture... in the Ute culture, there are stories about Coyote, wolf's younger brother. He's a trickster, but I'm rewriting him to be in present day, and he's going to be a thief who solves murders."

I nearly fell over. "You want to write mysteries?"

He nodded, clearly wondering if he'd said too much.

My suspicious thoughts brought back my guilt from earlier, but I went with them anyway. "Do you know what job I did before I moved to Estes Park?" Maybe he'd researched and found out that I'd owned Mystery Incorporated, a publishing company focused solely on various subgroups of the mystery genre.

He grimaced and gave me a reproachful stare. I could almost hear him think, *All right then, creepy old lady.*

I nearly laughed. "Okay, apparently not. Mystery novels happen to be my favorite, that's all."

Ben relaxed somewhat. "Oh. Mine too."

I glanced back at Watson, who stared up at me with his "*See? I know what I'm doing*" expression.

Maybe I'd regret it; maybe I wouldn't, but I didn't see how things could get much clearer. "Well, Ben, I wasn't quite prepared to hire anyone at this very moment, but why don't you come back in tomorrow, and I'll have all the paperwork figured out and printed off, and we'll go from there."

His eyes widened once more, and when he smiled, the scar on his lower lip grew more visible. "Really? I can work here?"

"Yes." Even as I spoke, a sense of calm came over me, that gut feeling that I'd come, lately, to trust. "As long as all the paperwork checks out and everything, you can probably start in a couple of days."

He practically glowed. "Thanks, lady!"

"You can call me Fred."

He cast me a puzzled expression, nodded, and then squatted down again. "Nice to meet you, Watson. I'll see you soon." He rubbed Watson's head again, stood, gave me a nervous wave and left the shop.

Watson watched him go, then grinned up at me before trotting off to his napping place.

"Oh no you don't. This was partially your fault."

He looked back at me over his shoulder.

"Actually, entirely your fault." I reached for his leash under the counter. "So you're coming with me."

ELEVEN

Maybe I was insane... probably no maybe about it, but at the thought of hiring Ben, the guilt I'd felt the entire day officially bubbled over. Even as I led Watson down the street toward Black Bear Roaster, my better senses tried to talk me out of it. And by better senses, I meant the lecture I'd gotten from Katie when I told her where I was going replayed in my mind.

I hadn't done anything wrong. I hadn't accused Carla of murdering her father-in-law. I hadn't caused her grandfather's seizures and couldn't be held responsible for his increased stress around the fear that I was going to. And it was utterly asinine to think I owed her any explanation for hiring her barista's twin brother.

Katie was right. And I knew it. Anyone with a lick of common sense knew it.

But still, it ate at me. I'd unintentionally been a thorn in Carla's side since I opted to have Katie make the top floor of my bookshop into a bakery. I wanted to start to smooth things out if I could, and letting her know up front that I was going to hire Ben, and reassure her that I wasn't trying to prove that she was a murderer, might start that process.

I supposed there was a chance I was wrong, that Carla had poisoned her father-in-law or, even if I was wrong and there was no poison, simply watched him choke to death on the floor at her feet.

That thought hadn't occurred to me before. I *could* actually see Carla doing the second option.

I shoved that notion aside easily as I weaved my way through the tourists moving at a snail's pace on the sidewalk. I couldn't clear the slate with her if I was wondering whether she'd rubbed her hands together and given a villain's laugh while watching Eustace Beaker choke to death on her dry, dry scones.

Watson and I were about three shops away from Black Bear Roaster when Harold walked out of the coffee shop.

I halted, stopping so abruptly that Watson jerked on his leash and glared back at me.

Harold appeared as sad and exhausted as he had that morning, though the bandages were off his face. It made him look worse, the freshly cleaned skin glossy with ointment over the superficial cuts. Behind him, Jonathan, holding what I assumed was a swaddled Maverick, exited the shop as well.

To my relief, the three of them headed in the opposite direction.

I waited for Carla to join them, but she didn't.

Had Harold been working, or had they simply been getting him out of Aspen Grove so he wasn't trapped in his room all day?

Surely he hadn't been working, not after his car wreck the day before. Even as I watched, it was easy to see he was moving stiffly, certainly sore. I was honestly surprised he'd been allowed to leave the retirement village at all. Well, Carla was a hard one to argue with when she got her mind made up.

The sight of Harold was nearly enough to make me change my mind, or come to my senses as Katie would've insisted. Nevertheless, I trudged on; Carla wasn't the only one who was stubborn. Maybe if I could convince Carla, she might convince Harold, and he could have some relief.

Black Bear Roaster was still fairly busy considering their bakery goods had killed a man a few short days ago. I caught sight of Carla's blonde hair as she walked from behind the counter and toward the backroom.

I considered following her, then rejected the idea. It would only seem like I was snooping. Especially after having been caught listening to her and Eustace the other day.

I'd wait it out. No need starting the conversation on the wrong foot.

We took our place in line behind two women. The older one was prim and, though I found her outfit garish, expensively dressed, while the younger was waifish and seemed rather scared.

Nick was the only one behind the counter, and his voice trembled as he addressed the older woman. "Apple cinnamon scone with apple butter, Ms. Apple?"

"Don't ask stupid questions, Nick. We're not in class at the moment. At least pretend that you can think on your own." Though her voice didn't raise, pure disdain dripped from every word.

"Sally..." The younger woman tentatively touched the other's arm. "Really, there's no call to—"

The prim woman, Sally Apple, apparently,

wheeled on her, eyes flashing. "Just because I'm forced to do weekly planning with you, does not mean I require your input on *anything*. Whether it be in the classroom, or a coffee shop, or anywhere else for that matter." She whipped back to Nick. "You tell me, *Mr. Pacheco*. Miss Morris and I come in here every week, at the exact same time, have the exact same thing—start off with our hot teas, and then the *exact* same thing halfway through. Furthermore, you know full well that Eustace had this particular scone put on the menu in honor of me. So... can you put two and two together now?"

It took all my willpower not to say something. To try to come to Nick's defense. But the combination of my own lingering guilt, shock at her vitriol, and feeling like I was back in the classroom of a truly horrible teacher, stole any words I might find.

Nick didn't reply to her, but simply retrieved two apple scones and spread apple butter on top of them. After he rung Miss Morris up, who paid for both scones, the women took their pastries and headed across the coffee shop to a table where a laptop sat beside a tower of notepads and a couple of over-flowing tote bags.

"Welcome back to Black Bear Roaster, Ms. Page.

What can I get you?" His cheeks were flushed and he didn't meet my eyes, clearly humiliated.

The last thing I planned on ordering was a scone. Though I had yet to sample anything that was moist and delicious, I was going to go for a cinnamon roll. However, the cinnamon rolls were in a large tray, and Nick would have to pull it out and then take time retrieving one. The jar of apple butter was still open behind him on the counter, so I decided to make it easy. Besides, surely the apple butter would help the scone be a little more edible. "I'll just take what they had, if you don't mind."

He nodded wordlessly, but before he could turn around, Sally Apple was back, shoving her plated scone between Nick and myself. "I thought I said to toast it. Same as every week, Nick. Rushing, just like you do on what little homework you actually accomplish."

He took the plate. "Sorry, Ms. Apple. I'll get you a fresh one."

I snagged the plate from his hand. "This will work for me. I don't need it toasted. Thank you."

Nick hesitated, then nodded, and went to work on a new scone, slicing it before putting it in the toaster.

I turned to the woman, unable to bite my tongue

any further. "If I'm understanding, you're one of Nick's teachers?"

She straightened her thin frame and turned slowly toward me like a perturbed robot, cast her glare down at Watson, who took a protected position behind my skirt, then back up. "Yes. Not that it's any of your business."

Though she was several inches shorter than me, I could feel myself wither under her stare, and to my surprise, my voice shook. "I had a teacher like you once. She was my English teacher. Spelling was a challenge, and she constantly told me how worthless I was. How I'd never be any good at writing." I hadn't even told my parents until the following year, though even then Dad stormed into the school and demanded her head on a platter. I lifted my voice to make sure Nick could overhear. "I went on to own my own publishing company, and now I own a book-shop. Despite having a hateful teacher such as yourself."

She lifted her chin, just slightly, and to my surprise the corner of her lips curved when she spoke and her words were calm and coated with ice. "That is an interesting story, Winifred Page. Funny how both of those careers require absolutely no writing at all. You published and now sell *other* people's words, not your own." She blinked. "Sounds like your teacher knew exactly what she was talking about."

Nick handed her a toasted and freshly buttered apple scone. "Sorry about that, Ms. Apple."

She didn't respond, didn't even look his way, just snatched the plate, lifted her chin slightly higher, and glided back to her table.

It wasn't until the younger teacher got my attention and shook her head slightly that I turned back to Nick. As I paid, I lowered my voice to a whisper. "I'm sorry. I wasn't thinking. Hopefully I just didn't make things worse for you when you're in her classroom."

He didn't respond, simply handed me back my credit card and then a pen to sign the receipt.

"But on a positive note, you've only got a couple more weeks to put up with her, right?"

He looked confused for a second and shook his head. "No. I'm not graduating until December."

Maybe I'd heard wrong. "Oh, sorry. I just met your twin. I was under the impression he was graduating at the end of May."

"He is. I'm not." Impossibly, he seemed even more ashamed and turned away.

I tried to find something to say, anything to make

it better, then decided the best thing to do was simply leave it alone.

I was certain, at this point, the best thing I could do would be simply to leave. But instead, I led Watson to a small table, as far away from Ms. Apple as I could possibly be, and sat down.

Still trying to think of a way to make Nick feel better, I took a bite of the scone and then cringed in surprise. Something was off, though I couldn't tell what it was. Maybe the apple butter was spoiled. I sniffed it. No, not spoiled. I smacked my lips. It hadn't tasted bad either, just not like apple butter.

The mystery was forgotten as Carla reentered the main space. She did a quick scan, her brows knitting as she noticed Nick's downcast expression, and then she froze when she saw me.

Her moment of indecision lasted only a second, and she stormed toward Watson and me, eyes blazing in fury.

Katie had been right. Common sense had been right. This had been a horrible, horrible idea.

Carla slammed both of her fists on top of the table and leaned toward me, her voice, though whispered, was sharp as knives. "You have some gall, Fred. How dare you come in here?" She leaned closer still, so near that I could feel the warmth of her breath wash over my cheeks. "Are you that incompetent of an amateur detective that you do your stakeout in broad daylight? What's your plan? Sit here with your stupid dog until I go crazy and start stabbing everyone?"

"No." I tried to keep my voice quiet as well. Clearly those around were aware of the scene, but the fewer people that overheard, the better. "I don't think that." I reconsidered the notion and raised my voice. "I don't think you killed your father-in-law, or anyone else. I've not said that to anybody."

She didn't miss a beat. "So you didn't go talk to Athena Rose the other day at the paper?" She sneered. "You didn't think I noticed you being all buddy-buddy with her that day? I bet you just loved it, taking my barista, and then palling around with a wannabe critic who wouldn't know good pastry items if they did the tango on her tongue?"

And once again, the realities of small-town life clarified in my mind. Of course someone had seen me going to the paper, and of course they'd gossiped about it. Couldn't even blame them, not after all I'd been involved in since moving to town.

"I promise you, Carla, none of that is how it looks to you. I hadn't even met Athena before that day. And I didn't talk to her at the paper to get dirt on you or your family." Though that was exactly what I'd gotten.

"Do you have any idea the stress you're causing my grandfather?" Clearly she wasn't interested in anything I had to say and wasn't going to believe it either way. "He's a mess thinking that you're going to try to pin Eustace's murder on me. His only grand-daughter. The mother of his only great-grandson. He can't take much more, in case him plowing through the store yesterday with my car didn't clue you in. And then you show up there this morning? Tell me you didn't go there hoping to get some dirt."

"No. I swear I..." My words trailed off, I couldn't lie to her. "I don't think you did it, Carla. I really don't."

"Like I care what you think." She straightened and pointed out the door. "Get out. You and your flea-ridden dog. Get out and don't ever come back."

I stood, and to my surprise, I realized I was trembling. Before I turned to leave, foolish or not, I decided to finish what I'd come here for, if for no other reason to avoid another altercation later. "I also wanted to let you know that Ben is going to start working for me at the bookshop."

She blinked and then shook her head. "Who in the world is Ben, and why would I care if he..." Realization dawned, and she glanced over at Nick. I was certain I'd just made his day markedly worse when I saw the fresh wave of hate in her eyes when she looked back. "Seriously, what is your damage? Do you have some sick fascination with being me? Trying to take over my life? What next? Are you going to adopt some baby and name him Maverick?"

There was a shattering of a plate behind us, cutting off my response, not that I'd figured out what I was supposed to say to that. We both turned to see Sally Apple stand so quickly that she bumped the table and knocked it over, eliciting more shattering of dishes. Papers went airborne from the table and books spread over the floor out of the tote bags.

The younger teacher screamed and jumped out of the way. "Help. Help us."

Sally clutched her throat and wheezed as she tried to suck in air. The sound was horrid. She seemed to be searching for something. Even as she attempted to breathe, she looked around the floor and her feet.

Miss Morris dropped to the ground as she continued to yell. She dug through the mass of books, papers, and tote bags, adding to the mess and chaos. "Her purse. We need her purse. Her EpiPen is in her purse."

Then it made sense. Allergic reaction to something.

Carla and I went into action at the exact same moment. She rushed toward them, yelling at the other customers. "You heard her, help us find Sally's purse. Now!" She raised her voice even louder. "Does anyone have an EpiPen? Anyone?"

I pointed over at Nick. "Call 911. Quickly."

He'd been frozen behind the counter, staring, but at my directive, picked up his cell and dialed the number.

No one had an EpiPen, but everyone began searching for Sally's purse, a few people were grabbing random purses and shoving them her way.

She shook her head, eyes wide as she continued struggling to breathe.

After a few more seconds, she went to her knees, and still no one could find her purse.

I rushed to her, though I had no idea what to do. She wasn't choking, she didn't need the Heimlich. I sank down beside her, and she fell over into my arms, still attempting to breathe, her flushed face starting to turn blue.

"Help is on the way, Sally. Help is on the way."

Miss Morris let out another yell from across the coffee shop. "Here it is!" She held up a purse from behind the counter, then rushed toward us, and dumped the contents in front of Ms. Apple and me.

She located the EpiPen and ripped off the lid, but it was too late.

Miss Morris stabbed the needle into Sally Apple's thigh, but it was still too late. Much too late.

TWELVE

A quiet shock filled Black Bear Roaster. After the chaotic cacophony of screams, choking, the shattering dishes, and the frantic search for Sally's purse, every single person remained frozen where they were. Even Watson did nothing more than press up against me.

When the ambulance and police arrived, things continued in slow motion. People spoke in whispers and seemed more confused than anything.

It had all been so sudden. So unexpected. And even to my own way of thinking, the thought felt strange, considering how much death I'd seen lately. But there was a difference between walking in on a dead body and holding a woman who was alive as she made the transition to death in your arms. One minute Sally Apple had been... well... a fairly miserable woman, if my short impression was correct, and then the next... she wasn't.

The police took statements as the first responders handled Ms. Apple. Interviews were hushed and slow. They took long enough that Watson and I were forgotten in the shuffle, and we sat in the corner by the wall and front window and simply observed. And thought.

Bananas.

That was the flavor when I'd bitten into the scone. I'd expected apple and gotten banana. When it felt like no one was looking, I lifted the plate I'd used and sniffed the scone with a solitary bite out of it. The combination of apple and banana.

Not that bizarre of a combination, I supposed, simply apple butter and banana butter. Bananas weren't my favorite fruit, but they weren't repugnant. But for Ms. Apple, it seemed, they were deadly. Unless... hers had been poisoned as well.

That didn't make any sense. I stood right there as Ms. Apple and Miss Morris had gotten their matching orders. In fact, I'd commandeered the first scone Sally Apple had received.

I eyed the pastry warily at that thought. Was it poisoned? Had my single bite simply not been enough to make me sick. Or... make me sick *yet*?

No sooner had the fear spiked than I shoved it

away as irrational. The scone wasn't poisoned. I was fine. As was Miss Morris, apparently.

Sally Apple couldn't have been poisoned. She simply died of anaphylactic shock. That and the result of misplacing her purse.

Maybe I had been wrong about Eustace. Maybe it had been the exact same thing. Now that I thought about it, I couldn't quite recall how he'd seemed when he'd choked before disappearing down the hallway. Had it been the same as Sally? Had Eustace been allergic? Although, surely, that severe of a banana allergy couldn't be that common.

The image of him choking did come back then. He hadn't had an apple scone or apple butter. His had been covered with powdered sugar.

I tried to bring the scene back. The entirety of it. What had been the same? What had been different? Maybe the answer lay in the similarities.

Both times the coffee shop had been crowded. Although it had been more so before. Both had involved scones, and both Eustace and Sally died within moments of eating a scone. So maybe... I glanced toward the display case and counter. At Nick Pacheco, ashen and worried. He'd been there on both occasions. As had Carla. The girl... Tiffany...

she'd been there before, as had Harold. But not this time. Neither of them.

So, once again, maybe it was Carla.

I studied Nick. Surely not. The boy seemed barely brave enough to string enough words together to form a sentence, let alone murder people.

"Her! Fred! I want her gone." Carla's raised, shrill voice shattered the solemn stillness of the place and my thoughts about her barista.

I turned to see her talking to Susan and pointing my way.

"I want her to leave. She came in here accusing and searching for excuses to call me a murderer. She's obsessed with me. Wants to take over my life." Carla paused long enough to sniff, wipe at her bangs, and then pointed again. "Get out of here! Get out of here!" She was edging toward hysteria.

There was no temptation to argue or defend myself. I wanted to do exactly what she asked.

Susan cast a glare at Branson, and he walked over from the person he was interviewing, took my arm, and leaned in close to whisper, "Probably a good idea. I'll come get your statement when I'm done here, if that's all right."

"Sure." I nodded and kept myself from looking over at Carla.

"You'll be at the bookshop?"

"Yes. I'll wait there."

I kept my gaze on the ground, furiously avoiding anyone else's inspection as I led Watson out of Black Bear Roaster. Probably for the last time.

"Bananas?" Katie took a bite of her lemon-and-lavender cupcake, sighed at the flavor, then returned her attention to me as I leaned on the counter. "Are we actually saying murder by banana? Is that a thing?"

It had been a few hours since Sally's death, and the bookshop and bakery had been slammed with people gathering to share the latest gossip. Business hours had come and gone, and I hung up the Closed sign on the door but left it unlocked so Branson could come in when he was finished. Katie and I hadn't had an opportunity to talk freely between the two of us.

"I don't know. I wouldn't think murder by banana would be a thing, but it looks like it. Unless it was just an accident." I started to take a bite of my almond croissant, then ripped off a small piece and tossed it to Watson instead. "But that seems like too much of a coincidence, doesn't it? Two deaths in

Black Bear Roaster in just a few days?" I leaned closer, bugging my eyes toward Katie. "Two deaths by scones... I mean, come on. That can't simply have happened randomly."

Katie hummed as she chewed and considered. Finally she swallowed and shrugged. "Well, they say bananas are the fruit of wise men." She lifted a finger. "And did you know that bananas don't technically grow on trees. That those '*trees*'"—she used her fingers to make air quotes—"are actually just herbs. They're in the same family as lilies and orchids."

I stared at her, and then burst out with a sardonic laugh. "Oh good grief, I thought you actually had a theory about what was going on at Carla's. What did you do this afternoon? Hop on Google between customers?"

She looked offended. "I would hope you know me better than that. You don't think my knowledge only comes from a frantic Google search and then it just disappears within half an hour, do you? I'm a well-read, well-studied individual, who is capable of retention of knowledge." She smirked.

I raised my hands in surrender, still chuckling. "All right, all right, I wasn't trying to imply anything derogatory. But I was expecting an actual thought about the case at hand, not just bananas at large."

"Fair enough." Katie took another large bite of the cupcake, chewed, and had almost swallowed it all before she started speaking again. "Just one more interesting tidbit, if you don't mind."

Watson growled softly and shuffled over to the top of the stairs leading down to the bookshop.

I glanced his way and then turned back to Katie as I rubbed my temples. "I know you'll probably explode if you don't get it out, so go ahead."

"That's more than likely true, yes." Katie finally swallowed the last of the cupcake and licked off lingering traces of icing from her lips. "Did you know that a banana is the fastest fruit to ever run a marathon?"

I blinked, and tried to decide if I'd heard her wrong, or if the exhaustion she had to feel from all the long hours was finally getting to her. "I'm sorry, did you just say that a *banana* ran a marathon? Do you sometimes use children's picture books in place of Google?"

"And again with the insults." Katie forced a serious expression, but the humor was evident in her tone. "It was a marathon in Barcelona where people dressed up as fruits and things. Patrick Wightman wore a banana costume when he ran the marathon in just under three hours. Officially making the banana the fastest fruit in long-distance running."

"You know, if I find out that discussions like these are what lead to you solving murders before we police can, I think I'm going to turn in my badge."

Katie and I looked over to see Branson turn from the stairway and head in our direction. He paused to pet Watson, who sidestepped him gracefully and trotted to his favorite table to nap under the window.

Branson narrowed his eyes at Watson's retreat and then refocused on Katie and me as he joined us at the bakery counter. "Please tell me that I'm not going to have to do any research into racing fruit to solve Sally Apple's death."

"Only if you're lucky." Katie grinned at him, then motioned toward the picked-over remains of that morning's baking. "Care for anything? The pecan pie bars are rather out of this world, if I do say so myself."

"Goodness, no." Branson's gaze traveled between Katie's empty plate and what was left of my almond croissant. "Got to hand it to you—you are two brave women eating pastries at a time like this."

"Well, today is full of insults it seems." Ignoring Branson's request, she plated up one of the bars. "I make everything here myself. And I'm very careful about when I put poison into something to remember which batch is the lucky winner." She slid the pastry toward him. "Now, as you fill us in, eat this in way of apology."

He considered the offering and then shrugged. "You know, Katie, if insulting you results in being force-fed your delicacies, I'm going to have to come up with an exhaustive list of ways to be offensive."

"Try it. Like I said, I remember where I put the poison." She watched as Branson slid a fork into the pecan bar and turned back to the pastry case. "There's only one of those left. I might as well make it none."

As Katie got the final pecan pie bar, I leveled my stare on Branson. "I take it you've determined that Sally was murdered?"

Unlike Katie, Branson made certain to swallow before he spoke. "No, not exactly. Tests will have to be done on all of that, and from what Miss Morris relayed, Sally truly did have a severe allergy to bananas."

"Obviously." Katie snorted, crumbs flying.

Branson gave her a sidelong glare and then shook his head like he was about to laugh. "The thing is, if anaphylactic shock truly is what killed her, it'll be a lot harder to prove that there was malicious intent than if she'd been poisoned." His green gaze flicked to me and held. "I actually had you on my list for this afternoon before we were called in to Black Bear Roaster."

"I was on your list?" Maybe I was reading into things, but I thought I caught the hint of the double entendre in his words.

Another flicker of a smile, though his words gave nothing else away. "Yes. I got the test results back on the first scone. You were right. It was poisoned."

I sucked in a breath, and my heart began to race. Though I would never admit it to him or anyone else, it beat in excitement. "Eustace was poisoned?" I'd been right. Even with all the guilt and beginning to think I was crazy, I'd been right.

"Yes." He nodded and then shrugged. "Kind of."

I balked. "Kind of? How does someone *kind of* get poisoned?"

Branson took another bite of the pecan pie bar, chewed, swallowed, then looked to Katie. "Poison or not, this is exceptional." Then he took another bite.

I swatted at him. "Knock it off."

He chuckled, but still insisted on finishing the chewing and the swallowing before the speaking "Well... the *scone* was poisoned, but Eustace didn't die from it. He truly did choke. The poison didn't have any time to take effect at all. Though, it would've. Eustace would've had a pretty painful death within a day or so."

Eustace had choked. Just like it seemed. Just like everyone had said.

But he'd also been poisoned, just like my gut told me—even though it made absolutely no sense. I wasn't quite sure what to do with that. "Okay then, what does that make it? An accident or murder?"

He shrugged again. "Eustace Beaker died from choking; *that* was an accident. But someone out there is guilty of attempted murder."

"So, just like with Sally Apple, maybe the bananas in the apple butter might have been accidental but resulted in an actual murder." Katie took a large, rather emphatic bite of the pecan bar.

"Possibly." He waffled his hand. "That's not exactly how I'd put it, but still. We're going to have to test all the jars of apple butter. Maybe there was a mix-up at the factory. It really could just be an accident."

"An accident? You just told me that there was poison in Eustace's scone. That's not an accident, regardless of how he actually died. Someone was trying to kill him. You really think it's a possibility that Sally just happened to die due to another scone within a couple of days?"

"Anything is a possibility." He didn't sound like he believed it. "Regardless, like you said, someone was trying to kill Eustace. That's true whether Sally's death was an accident or not. Although, I'm not placing money on her purse containing an EpiPen *accidentally* being misplaced behind the counter. Ergo, if Sally's death wasn't an accident, then I would imagine the two would have to be connected. That really would be too large of a coincidence to have two different murderers choose to use Carla's scones in the same week. I just have to figure out who it is that had it out for Eustace. And we all know that list isn't going to be short."

"Any ideas on who might be near the top of that extensive list?" I couldn't help myself.

"No, Fred. I just got the results an hour before the latest crisis you were a part of." He held up his hand and smiled when I started to protest. "I was also planning on telling you this next part so I could prove what I promised. Especially considering I wouldn't have tested the scone if it hadn't been for you to begin with. As long as you're not in the police's way or committing crimes, I'm not going to stop you from snooping around. You were right, and you've more than helped before. I'm sure you will again."

I wasn't certain what to do with that. After a couple of days of increasing guilt and feeling like I was seeing shadows where there were none, that bit of validation and trust was overwhelming, and greatly needed. I simply nodded, slowly, taking it all in and not finding any other words to say.

"I will offer one... warning, I suppose." His tone sounded questioning. "Maybe piece of advice would be a better phrase. I'd give Carla some space. I'm not sure if you really think she's a suspect or not, but if things do start pointing to her in your mind, I'd rather you tell me and let us handle it. I don't see Carla as a murderer, but with the way she's feeling about you right now, a confrontation between the two of you might result in a rather ugly scene."

I didn't even have to consider. "I agree. Carla needs her space from me, and I plan on giving it to her."

Branson's eyebrows popped up, as if he'd been expecting an argument. "Okay, then. Great." His expression grew nervous, which was unusual for Branson, and finally he glanced at Katie. "Would you mind plugging your ears or looking the other way or something. I'm going to ask Fred on another date, and I'd rather do that in private."

Katie jumped, flushed, and then giggled. "You bet. In fact, I've heard rumors that the shop downstairs contains cookbooks. And goodness knows I don't have enough recipes. I think I'll go hunting." She winked at me and made a show of scurrying around the counter and then out of the bakery.

My heart began to race for an entirely different reason. "Is this how you treat every murder investigation? With invitations to dinner?"

"Like there's another choice with you involved." He reached out and took hold of my arm lightly. "Would you go out with me again, maybe this weekend or something? We could try a restaurant that actually cooks our food for us this time. You know, something wacky and untraditional like that."

I was on dangerous ground. Even though there'd been several months break between us going out before and the steakhouse, they were starting to add up. Soon there would be expectations, reasonably so. That meant I'd have to quit wondering about what I felt for Branson, quit wondering about what I felt for Leo. Quit wondering about what Leo and Katie felt for each other. I'd simply have to decide what I wanted. If anything.

Branson withdrew his hand and looked hurt. "Probably not a good sign that asking you out prompts a wave of stress so strong it nearly knocks me over."

"No. I'm sorry." That time I reached out and touched his arm. "I'd love to go to dinner. Again." Sure enough, excitement and stress flared in equal measure. Maybe another dose of honesty would ease my nerves. "Just remember. I need to go slow. Very slow. I wasn't planning on ever having a relationship again, and I'm not entirely sure if I want one."

Those green eyes stared into mine, patiently, and I could swear, hopefully. And he waited.

"But... I'm not entirely sure that I don't want one either."

He smiled gently. "Slow works for me, Fred." He leaned in, then pressed a very quick, very soft kiss to my lips and pulled back. "In the meantime, be careful snooping. If the same person who poisoned Eustace is responsible for Sally, then we've got someone who's most definitely not afraid to stack up some bodies. Someone who seems to be capable of doing it stealthily too."

After pigging out on Katie's pastries, I went home and made Watson's nightly baked chicken, and after a longing near-romance with the pasta in the cupboard, opted for baked fish for myself. The recipe I used was good enough, but it was still baked fish. Not overly satisfying, but guilt free. I'd never had a waifish figure, but having a bakery above my head, while delicious, hadn't been helpful. There needed to be cuts somewhere.

After dinner, I studied my overstuffed armchair sitting near the fireplace. I could open all the windows and let in the cool May evening air to compensate for building a fire to make it cozy while I read. Any other night, that was exactly what I would do. It was one of the reasons I wasn't sure I wanted another relationship. I enjoyed my time on my own—just Watson, me, and a good book. I was certain most people would think that sounded sad, but I didn't. After Garrett's and my divorce, spending my evenings reading was the epitome of freedom.

I couldn't make myself do it. Couldn't curl up in the comfortable armchair and get lost in a story. Not after having Sally Apple die in my arms just a few short hours before. My guilt over stressing out Carla's grandfather and wondering if I was crazy for suspecting poison was gone, but in its place was a weighty sense of melancholy.

Watson was already curled up at the base of the armchair, ready for our nightly routine, but instead of slipping into pajamas, I put my boots back on and walked to the door, smacking my thigh. "Come on, buddy. Let's go get ice cream."

Yes, ice cream. I'd had baked fish, after all. I wasn't a masochist.

Though there were several mom-and-pop ice cream parlors in downtown, one of the few chains Estes Park allowed was Dairy Queen, for whatever reason. And I was glad. There were moments like this where the taste of my Midwest childhood was required.

I ordered a large Oreo Blizzard. Seeing as I'd also scarfed down a salad alongside the baked fish, I had them put two servings of cookie dough in it, as well.

Watson got an empty cake cone and was beyond thrilled.

Holding Watson's leash loosely in my hand and with a death grip on my Blizzard, we strolled up and down the river walk that ran behind the shops. The evening was in the low sixties, and my thick sweater had been more than enough. However, the ice cream was leaving me chilled, even if pleasantly satiated.

Coming into town had been the right call. A few tourists strolled lazily along the river walk as well, offering a sense of camaraderie, and their quiet conversations were muffled by the comforting tumult of the river tumbling over boulders and rocks. The sky was cloudless and congested with stars over the peaks of the mountains that surrounded Estes. Despite the frequency of murderers, the town was a little haven.

With the Blizzard half gone, I paused our walk as we drew next to the parking lot once more and leaned on the railing that overlooked a particularly low point in the rushing river. With the quiet sounds of nature and the familiar ice cream of my childhood on my tongue, it was almost like my father was beside me. I often felt like that. Though I'm sure others would find the belief superstitious and flighty, I had no doubt Watson himself had been a gift from my father, so in a way, Dad was always with me. But more so in that moment.

He didn't offer any words, but I could feel his wheels turning alongside mine. I easily recalled the nights as a kid that I listened to him go over the details of cases he was working on, either talking to himself, Mom, or my uncles when they visited. And when I was quite a bit older, him asking my advice and thoughts on things that had him stumped. Looking back, I'm sure there were all sorts of details he'd left out due to my age, gory details he wouldn't have wanted his child to know of the world. At the time, though, I'd felt like I was his partner in crime. Or... his partner in solving crime.

I wondered what he would make of the double death by scones.

If he was there, he didn't whisper any answers or offer any clues. Although, knowing him, he was enjoying watching his daughter mull it over.

As I finished the rest of the Blizzard, I didn't come up with any answers either. The only thing I was certain of, was that the list of people who despised Eustace was long and rambling. I was willing to bet, if my brief impression of her was correct, that Sally Apple would be in the same predicament.

Finally, when the chill from the soft breeze combining with the ice cream became unpleasant, I decided I was being silly and we might as well return home. It was often the case that when I distracted myself with a book or busied myself with a task, things had a way of working themselves out in the back of my mind. Maybe that would happen with the windows open, the fire roaring, and a book on my lap.

I'd just opened the car door and allowed Watson to jump inside when there was a squeal of delight from somewhere behind me. I turned to find Carl and Anna Hanson hurrying our way. The older couple owned a luxury home-furnishings store directly across from the Cozy Corgi. Each of them held a towering chocolate-dipped ice cream cone.

"Winifred!" Anna threw her arms around me, pulled me into a quick, squishy embrace before practically shoving me aside so she could lean into my car toward who she considered my better half. "Watson, baby doll. How Mama has missed you. Aren't you just the—" Her words broke off as she sucked in a breath and then coughed. She practically threw herself backward to extricate herself from the car, waved a hand in front of her face as she attempted to breathe and then began spitting and pulling things off her tongue. She shoved the chocolate-dipped ice cream cone toward her husband. "Carl, get the dog hair off this while I try to clear it out of my mouth."

If it had been anybody else, I probably would've crawled into a hole out of embarrassment. Only a select few were allowed in my car, and that was only with the strict understanding that they would be covered in dog hair for the following month.

As I knew she would, once she'd gotten the hair out of her mouth, Anna dove back in, this time not speaking but lavishing vigorous physical affection on Watson. He was a good sport about it. Anna wasn't his favorite person in the world, but she typically came with a bevy of treats.

Carl held his nearly foot-tall chocolate-dipped ice cream cone toward me. "Would you hold this please?" Once I took it from him, he went to work removing the traces of corgi from Anna's ice cream.

After another minute or two, Anna emerged once more among a fresh cloud of dog hair. She waved her hand in front of her face, paused smartly as the hair drifted away before she dared to suck in another breath and shook her finger at me. "You've only had this car a matter of weeks. How in the world could you let it get so bad?"

I shrugged, unapologetic. "I vacuum it out every

week. That's life with a corgi. You should see under my bed when I forget to use the vacuum attachment after a while. You would think I had a whole battalion of corgis, from the looks of it."

Carl handed the cone back to Anna. I doubted he'd had long enough to remove all the hair, but Anna didn't seem to mind. He dug in his pocket with his newly freed hand, pulled out his cell, and flicked on the light as he aimed it at the car. "I forgot you got a new Mini Cooper. I'm glad you didn't change; it suits you." He leaned closer and then looked up in surprise. "But you got the same color? I thought maybe you'd mix it up since the insurance paid for you to get a new one."

Katie and I had been run off the road a couple months before. We'd survived, but my other Mini Cooper hadn't. "You sound nearly as disappointed as Katie did when she saw it for the first time. She was almost angry about it. But it's not the same color. My original one was a burnt orange. That option isn't available now. This one is called *volcanic* orange. It's a little brighter." I tapped the top of my new beloved Mini Cooper. "Of course, Katie says it looks like spicy mustard, but I like it."

Carl didn't seem convinced. Neither did Anna. She took a bite of her ice cream cone, then shook her head. "You shouldn't be so resistant to change, dear. It's good for the soul."

It'd taken me a while, but I'd learned to truly care about Carl and Anna. Plus, they were tied with Percival and Gary for first place as the biggest gossips in town. Maybe their timing was perfect. But Anna was always full of advice, so I decided to cut her off before she launched into a lecture, which somehow I was certain would begin with the color of my Mini Cooper and end up with pressuring me to get engaged to Branson or Leo. "I haven't seen you two in several days. Any new pictures of that grandson of yours?" I couldn't remember his name, but he'd been born around the same time as Carla's son, and I wasn't above using him as a segue. He lived in Florida, but their daughter sent them daily pictures and videos.

Without missing a beat, Carl switched the phone from flashlight to photo album, and for the next five minutes—as Watson curled up and went to sleep on the passenger seat—we looked at pictures of Timothy, who they constantly referred to as Tiny Tim. Maybe I hadn't forgotten his name so much as intentionally blocked it out.

With much *oohing* and *aahing*, from all three of us, Carl finally reached the end with a photo their daughter had sent of Tiny Tim spitting up his dinner from an hour ago. I was glad I'd finished my Blizzard, but Carl and Anna continued their enthusiastic enjoyment of what remained of their ice cream cones.

"He is a beautiful baby. It's clear how proud you both are, rightly so." I left the driver's side door open so Watson had fresh air, and I leaned against the hood of the car with Carl on one side and Anna on the other. One of the beautiful things about the couple was that they required no subtlety whatsoever. "I'm assuming you heard about what happened at Black Bear Roaster this afternoon?"

Both of their eyes went wide and grins spread across their faces that assured me I'd just given them a treat a thousand times better than ice cream.

Anna clutched one hand at the bosom of her gingham dress as she spoke. "Of course we did. The whole town heard. How could they not? We also heard you were there. And that you were also there when Eustace died." Though she shook her head in what was probably meant to be sympathy, she didn't bother to try to make it convincing. "I have to say, we were really upset that we missed that one. Well, both of them. All that excitement and there we were just a few doors down not selling a lick of furniture because everyone else was watching the show firsthand."

"Anna! Really!" As he sometimes did, Carl took a little longer than his wife to get into the swing of things. I had yet to figure out why he bothered, but at times, he liked to appear above it all. "You're talking about two people who lost their lives. Perhaps we should show a little more decorum?"

Anna had finished what was left of her ice cream cone a few moments before, and she reached out and snagged the inch of what remained of Carl's cone. "Oh, shut up. Eustace and Sally were miserable human beings. Absolutely miserable. We were two of the lucky ones who managed to stay in their good graces, but it was a high-wire at times." She turned back to me with a knowing look, the lights of the Dairy Queen sign at my back washing her features away in a red glow. "They both liked to be in charge of *everything*. Granted, Eustace Beaker sort of *was* in charge of everything, but Sally Apple was in charge of enough, let me tell you. However—" She popped the bottom part of Carl's cone into her mouth and kept going "—she did like to redecorate her home every few years, so she was good for business. I will miss that."

"Oh." Carl's shoulders slumped, and he joined

me by leaning on the hood of my car. "I didn't even think about that aspect. She'll be hard to replace."

Anna nodded in agreement but brightened quickly. "Rumor is, you suspect Carla of murdering Eustace. Can't say I blame her; he was horrible to her just like everyone else. Never good enough for his son. Not for someone with the Beaker name. Of all people, no one in town believed when Jonathan Beaker, who never showed an ounce of spine his entire life, defied his parents and married the White girl. The Whites always were considered a little low-class." She waved her hand in the air, stopping me as if I'd been about to interrupt. Silly, as I knew better. "Of course *we* didn't think that. In fact, Dolana was the sweetest thing you can imagine. Dolana was Carla's grandmother. I guess technically, she wasn't a White at all; she married into the family just like Jonathan did. But she was a good one. And there's nothing wrong with Harold, I suppose. There's just not much to him." As if to prove what a rock star in the world of gossip she was, Anna surged ahead, not needing to stop for breath. "But Dolana's family wasn't that much higher up on the food chain than the Whites, so that marriage wasn't quite so shock-ing. But for Jonathan Beaker..." She *tsked*. "Well, I know that was before your time, but let me tell you, that was a *scandal*. Like the prince marrying the little pauper girl. And don't you think, not even for one second, that Eustace Beaker ever let Carla forget it. Why, if I was her, I would have shoved my too-dry scones down his throat and held his mouth and nose shut years ago."

It seemed word about the poison hadn't spread yet.

"I would've too." Apparently, Carl had decided to join in on the fun. "Take us, for example. We're not in love with our son-in-law. He's a little bit like Harold. There's just nothing to him really; he's a bit of a cardboard cutout, truth be told. But our daughter loves him, so that's enough. We would never treat him as if he was a second-class citizen in our family. Even though he is. But he doesn't know that."

When there was finally a break, I dared to speak. "I heard that rumor myself, that I was suspecting Carla. But I wasn't, not really."

"Oh." Anna and Carl spoke in unison and had matching expressions of disappointment on their faces. Anna recovered quicker. "Well, with Eustace, you'll have no shortage of suspects."

I did love how they just assumed, by this point, that not only was I looking into things, but that I'd figure them out. "What about Sally Apple? I only met her once, but she seemed rather—" I considered sugarcoating, then remembered who I was talking to. "—malicious. I was disgusted with how she treated that poor barista, Nick. I guess he's a student of hers, and she absolutely berated him in front of the entire coffee shop."

And again, as if they shared one mind, Anna and Carl moved as one, both straightening, eyes widening, as they glanced at each other and nodded.

"What?" I wasn't sure what I'd just said.

"*That's* your other suspect. I wondered." Anna smiled at me in approval. "You're a quick one."

Carl patted me on the shoulder. "Sally's probably not even cold yet, and you've figured out who killed her."

Maybe it was brain freeze from the ice cream, but it took me noticeably too long to catch up. "Nick? You think Nick did it?" He was a possibility, but I just couldn't see it happening. Though Carl and Anna seemed convinced. I had to remind myself that less than a heartbeat ago they'd both been confident it had been Carla.

"Well, of course he did." Anna rolled her eyes, like it was the most obvious thing in the world. "It's because of Sally that Nick's not graduating on time.

Not even graduating with his twin." Her expression saddened, and her tone became a little more genuine. "Those boys have had a rough go of it. They both seem sweet. Odd and a little shy, but that's how twins can be." She paused and patted my hand. "Look who I'm talking to. You know that more than anyone. Given your stepsisters and their husbands. But still, it hurt my heart a little bit to know that Nick wouldn't be able to graduate with Ben. Didn't seem fair."

"Well, I betcha Sally regrets that choice now. Doesn't she?" Carl joined in on his wife's solemnity.

"Good point." Anna nodded in agreement and folded her hands as if in respect for the dead.

I just couldn't see it. Although, they always say it was the quiet ones you have to watch out for. And Nick definitely had opportunity for both. Plus, I could only imagine how Eustace had treated him. Now here was further motive of why he'd want to harm Sally Apple, besides her being a belittling teacher.

Once more I remembered who I was talking to, and knew I needed to make clear my thoughts on Nick before it was spread around town by noon the following day like it was the gospel truth that Winifred Page had accused the barista of murder. "I suppose he's a possibility, but I'm not convinced. Like you said, lots of people had reason to hate Eustace Beaker. And it sounds like the same is true for Sally."

"Well, that's very true. *Very*." Carl rubbed his bald head. "She had a reputation all over town, and that's not even including all of the students' lives she's made miserable throughout the years. *And* their families."

"You're right!" Anna reached across me and smacked Carl's arm. "That brings us to Carla once more. Sally held her back a year too. Maybe revenge is best served cold, and dry."

"Maybe." Suddenly Carl sounded less certain. "But like I said, that list is huge. She was a nightmare to Alice's son; she's talked a lot about it in bird club. And think about Odessa. She was on track to be valedictorian until she took Sally's class. I thought Athena was going to murder her for that. Oh, oh." He waved both his hands excitedly in the air. "And remember what she did to Declan Diamond his senior year?" His brows knitted suddenly. "Oh, never mind. I guess he's not a suspect. He's dead."

My heart stopped, and I reached out slowly and touched Carl's arm, right where Anna had slapped him moments before. "Did you say Athena? Athena Rose?"

He nodded.

Anna took over the storytelling. "Odessa is Athena's granddaughter. A brilliant, gorgeous girl. She's a star on Broadway now. But Sally Apple took a dislike to her." Anna leaned in to whisper by my ear, though we were surrounded only by parked cars. "Everyone thought it was because Sally didn't want a black girl to be valedictorian." She pulled back slightly and gave me the evil eye before returning to normal volume. "No matter what assignment Odessa did for Sally, she gave her bad marks. Every time. Athena complained to the principal, threatened to sue, but Sally and Eustace go way back. Several of the ones on the town council do. The principal's hands were tied unless he wanted to be out of a job."

And another bombshell. "Sally was on the town council?"

They both nodded. This time, it was Carl whose eyes brightened with an idea. "Not anymore. I hadn't even thought of it; there're two vacant seats. Maybe it's time for Carl Hanson to be a town leader."

"And why not me?" Anna sounded truly offended, and seemed on the verge of smacking Carl again, although this time much less playfully.

"Hold on." I put out both of my hands, touching each of them on the arm. "There are *two* spots. Maybe you two can be a power couple."

They seemed to consider and then relaxed. Crisis averted. But the suggestion triggered a wave of speculation and excitement. And for the next twenty minutes, I was privy to all the ways Anna and Carl would change the town if they got into power.

Occasionally, I glanced over, envying Watson taking his peaceful nap, but most of what they said flitted past. I was too preoccupied with options I hadn't really considered. Perhaps I'd discounted Athena too quickly. Or, maybe, Anna and Carl weren't the only ones who thought it was time for a change in town leadership. It was possible Eustace and Sally hadn't been killed because they were horrible and mean, but simply because they had powerful positions someone else wanted.

FOURTEEN

"You think somebody might be making their way through the town council?" Katie didn't pause in her preparations. We opened in less than half an hour, but I'd come upstairs to fill her in on my conversation with Carl and Anna from the night before.

"It's a possibility." I took a sip of the dirty chai Katie had taken the time to prepare for me and did my best to ignore Watson's accusatory, yet pleading, stare between me and the pastry case. I wasn't allowing myself to have any treats either after our late-night ice cream run, and the smell of Katie's baking was delicious torture.

"If you're right—" Katie was interrupted by the buzzing of an alarm. She hurried over, turned off the oven, and pulled out a pan of chocolate croissants before starting over. "If it is about the town council, then that means there's, what? Three more people on the kill list?"

"Four. I think there are six members. But maybe it's another one of the council members who's doing the murdering. Working their way up, or enacting a vendetta."

Katie considered as she popped another tray of pastries into the oven. "I vote for someone outside the town council. Granted, I don't know them all individually, but what little I've heard about them, they sound like they make a lot of people miserable. Unless you're one of their favorites, they add a lot of pressure to starting up a business in town."

My gut said she was right about that, considering all the things I'd heard from Paulie. "It's definitely a theory worth considering. The thing I don't understand is why they would use Carla's coffee shop as their weapon of choice for the first two murders. Unless they also have some grudge against Carla and they're either trying to frame her or push her out of business."

Katie straightened, cocked an eyebrow, and grinned expectantly.

"What?"

"The way you said that, Fred. You managed a straight face. As if you couldn't imagine why someone would ever possibly hold a grudge against Carla? I'd say she has nearly as many people in town who have a problem with her as her father-in-law did."

Well, there was that. "You may be right, but there seems to be a difference between the two of them. Carla just has a temper and is..." *How in the world to sum up Carla?*

"Kind of mean?" Katie shrugged as if simply trying to be helpful.

"Sure. Kind of mean." She wasn't wrong. "But it's a different flavor than Eustace. From what I'm learning about Sally, different from her, too. Both had positions of power and used them to hurt or hold back others. Carla doesn't do that."

"I suppose that's true." Katie paused in her task, leaning against the counter as she met my gaze. "You have another thought. I can hear it. You think the town council is a possibility, but it doesn't feel right to you?"

I studied her. "I don't know if it's comforting or disconcerting that you know me so well."

Instead of answering, she went to the pastry case and retrieved a freshly baked pumpkin scone. "I know you've been eyeing this too. Quit counting calories and enjoy yourself." Before she shoved it my way, she broke off the corner and tossed it to Watson.

He gave a little hop, caught it, and waddled away happily.

"You know you're going to have to use all of your profits to buy me a new wardrobe when I can't fit into anything in my closet."

"Money well spent." She smacked the countertop. "No price is too high to get you out of those drab baby-poop colors you love so much."

"I'd call you a bad name right now if you hadn't just given me a scone." I took a bite and closed my eyes to savor for a second before continuing. "You're right, however. I can't keep from thinking about Athena. She had more than an ample motive to want Eustace dead. She said as much. She hated the man. But I'm willing to bet she hated Sally Apple more. It's one thing for somebody to hurt you; it's another when they go after your family, especially a kid or grandchild."

Katie grimaced. "I don't want to think of her like that. I really like Athena."

"Me too."

Katie brightened. "That doesn't make any sense on why she would use Carla's, though."

"Doesn't it? It was her review of the coffee shop that made Eustace take away the job she really wanted at the paper, and made it where she couldn't do it anywhere else in town."

"Oh, right. I forgot." Her expression fell again. "I don't want it to be her, though. I want it to be another town council member. One of the ones who gave Paulie such a hard time when he was opening his pet shop."

"Really?" That surprised me. "I didn't know you and Paulie—"

A loud knocking cut me off.

Watson let out a yelp and ran to the top of the steps, then glared back at me as if wanting to know why I was moving so slowly.

The knocking became banging.

"Well, that's unusual." Katie began to walk around the counter. "Either someone's in desperate need of caffeine, or something is up."

"I'll check. You've got lots of work to do. You don't have to come." I headed toward Watson.

"Right, that's how this is going to play out. Two people died from scones, and everyone in town knows Winifred Page has a knack for finding out who killed who. You may need more than a corgi as your bodyguard."

"If someone was coming to hurt me, I hardly think they'd knock." I reached Watson but didn't put up any more protest. Katie had a point. If somebody wanted to hurt me, as devoted as Watson might be, I might require more than a cute, moody ball of dog treats and fluff to come to my aid.

The silhouetted form peering into the front door became clearer as we approached.

Katie paused a few feet away. "We were just talking about Nick a few minutes ago. A little strange that he'd show up."

I spared her a glance. "You worked with him for a while. He doesn't make you nervous, does he? I always got the sense that you liked him."

"I did, a lot. I do. He's hard to get to know. I think more than anything, I feel sorry for him, but"—she shrugged—"let's be careful."

"I always am." I ignored Katie's scoff and unlocked the door. "Nick, what in the world are you doing...?" I noticed the scar on his lip and realized my mistake. "Oh. Ben, hi. I was going to call you tonight about the job. Don't you have school this morning?"

He stepped past me, not waiting for an invitation. "I skipped it. I needed to see you."

Ben halted as he noticed Katie and Watson. Then he stuck out his hand. "Hey, I'm Ben, Nick's brother. We never met. You're Katie, right? He always talked about how nice you were when you worked together."

Katie accepted the handshake and visibly relaxed. "I don't know how anyone could be anything but nice to Nick. He's a sweetheart."

"That's exactly why I'm here. Nick is—" He stopped when Watson nudged his shin with his head. It appeared there was a third man in Watson's life who'd somehow won his affection. Ben bent down, murmuring softly to Watson as he stroked his head, and smiled gently. He only took a few moments before standing, his expression turning serious once more. "The police arrested Nick this morning for Mr. Beaker and Ms. Apple's deaths."

Perhaps it shouldn't have surprised me, but it did, somehow. And there was a twinge of something at his words. I couldn't quite tell what it was. Some combination of irritation that I hadn't determined the killer before the police and that I misjudged Nick so poorly. I considered myself better at reading people than that.

Katie and I exchanged glances, neither of us sure what to say.

"Oh. I see." Ben looked back and forth between us. Despite how easygoing he'd seemed the other day, I saw clear frustration that transitioned to condemnation in his eyes. "I expected more of you than that." His lips moved silently before he found words again. "I thought you were different. Thought you'd see past all the whispered rumors about us."

I took a step forward. "Ben, I haven't heard any rumors. At least nothing outside of Nick being held back because of Ms. Apple's class, and knowing that Mr. Beaker didn't treat him very well."

He clearly didn't believe me. Again, it seemed like he was struggling with what to say, then shook his head and started to walk past me. "Never mind. Clearly I was wrong."

Without thinking I reached out and grabbed his wrist before he got to the door. "Wait. I'm not sure how we upset you. What did you want to say?"

He shook his head once more, started to walk off, then paused. "Everybody knows that you solve murders. I came here to ask you to figure out who killed those two people and clear my brother's name. I swear to you he didn't do it. He never would." His brown eyes searched mine, and then his lips thinned. "But you don't believe me. Why would you?" That time he did jerk his arm free and stormed from the shop.

Watson whined, and trotted along the window, following Ben's trail until he disappeared from view.

Katie and I simply stood, frozen, then stared at each other. Katie spoke first. "I agree with him, Fred. Whether he had reasons or not, he couldn't do it. He just wouldn't."

I nearly laughed. "You were just saying we should be careful if we let him in."

"I know. And I'm ashamed of that now." Her cheeks flushed. "If anybody should know better than to listen to rumors and judge a kid from them, it should be me."

"*You've* heard rumors about Nick?"

She nodded. "About the Pacheco family in general. But it does seem Nick is the one most often singled out—the quieter one, the weirder one."

"You never mentioned it. Even when I told you I was thinking I was going to hire Ben."

She let out a frustrated breath. "I know. And I've been debating on it, but I decided not to say anything. For those very reasons. They're just rumors. Like I said, we both know that there've been plenty of rumors about me. And they weren't true. A kid shouldn't have to pay for their parents' mistakes."

"What are the rumors?" I couldn't help myself.

Katie's eyes narrowed, and I could see her stubborn streak rising to the surface. A quality we both shared.

"He's been arrested, Katie, for two murders. Surely whatever rumors you've heard aren't as big as that."

"You're right." She sighed as her shoulders slumped. "Rumors of dealing drugs, being the outcast. You know, all the rumors that go along with a kid anytime they're different or seem sad and quiet. Like they expect him to have a list of fellow students who've been mean to him and is just waiting to get revenge on."

In one way, from the brief glimpses I'd had of him, I could sort of understand that generalization, but still. "I just spoke to the king and queen of gossip last night. They didn't mention anything about that. How in the world do you know gossip they don't?"

"Anna and Carl aren't kids; they're not in school. There were some things Tiffany mentioned when I worked at Black Bear Roaster. She didn't believe them, but she didn't exactly stand up for him at school, either."

Even if they weren't in school, I was certain with Nick being arrested, all the adults in the town were about to be privy to whatever rumors their children were spreading about Nick, true or not. "Your gut says he didn't do it?"

It looked like Katie started to nod but caught herself. "Doesn't yours?"

"I don't know. My gut has been a mess lately. I kept thinking that—" I realized what I was about to say a heartbeat before I said it. I'd thought Eustace had been poisoned, when he choked, as if that was proof my guts weren't trustworthy. But I'd been right. How had I forgotten that so soon? I blinked, shook to clear my head, and then met Katie's gaze. "Yeah. It does."

"You've gotta be kidding me, Fred." Branson's voice on the other end of the line sounded more exasperated than anything.

"I'm just saying I think there are some other angles to consider besides Nick. In fact…" I paused as a couple of people entered the Cozy Corgi, but they walked past me with a small wave and joined the rest of the crowd that was gathering in the bakery. With the Black Bear Roaster closed until further notice, everyone was going to Katie's. I was certain it would be a good hour or two until anyone thought about shopping for books, so I'd taken the time to call Branson.

"In fact what?" Though he still sounded exasperated, I didn't catch any irritation in his tone.

"Sorry. People were walking by, and I didn't want to be overheard." I regathered my thoughts. "What I was going to say is, I think there are some other options. I didn't realize that Eustace and Sally were both on the town council. Maybe this is more of a town council issue than something revolving around the coffee shop."

He paused for long enough that for a moment I wondered if we'd lost the connection. "Fred, I do respect you, and I'm truly impressed by your skills and instincts. But I need you to give me a little credit here. Just because you didn't know they were both on the town council doesn't mean that I wasn't aware of that fact. I know you've beaten the Estes Park Police Department in solving the last few murders, but that doesn't prove we're complete morons."

All right, maybe I was picking up on some irritation. Before my own temper flared, I realized that he had a point. I also managed to catch my next instinct in time to keep from bringing up my suspicions of Athena Rose. I didn't want to throw someone else under the bus before I gathered more proof or facts, if there were any to be found.

"Fred? Are you still there?"

"Yeah. Sorry." Now I was on the phone with him, I wasn't sure what to say. Or, even why I'd called. Had I really expected to call and tell him that my gut told me Nick hadn't committed the murders and he'd go, *Sure, fine, I'll release him right now.* "He didn't do it, Branson. I can just feel it. Something doesn't add up." Apparently, I *could* tell him that it was simply a gut feeling.

"That's all you've got? You just know? Can you at least explain *what* doesn't add up?"

I didn't figure out what to say quickly enough, and he launched in again.

"From what I've gathered, Nick is one of those troubled kids, Fred. I know it's awful to think that someone so young could already be past saving, but maybe that's the case with him. He's been on our radar for a while. Hadn't found any proof up until this point, but I wish we had. Could have prevented some deaths."

"What proof do you have that he did this now?" I was the one sounding irritated. The tenor of my own voice only caused the sensation to grow as I knew I seemed irrational.

"Oh, come on." A small laugh burst from him, a dark one. "It's a long list. He was there for both murders, and there're eyewitnesses who can testify to him serving Sally the scone. Of which, you are one, unless you've forgotten." I could practically see him in my mind, numbering things off on his fingers. "Sally's purse with the EpiPen was behind the counter. She wouldn't have put it there. Someone else had to have done so. He could've easily slid it off the counter while she and Miss Morris were ordering. And Nick, just like all the students, knew about her banana allergy. It was severe enough that it was talked about with students and parents so they didn't bring any banana products into the classroom, ever. Banana was found in three of the jars of apple butter. Those jars had his fingerprints on them."

It was the first thing I thought I could argue with and I jumped on it. "He works there, of course his fingerprints were on them." Even as I said it, my conviction began to waver.

"Oh, Fred, come on." He sighed and for a second he reminded me of my ex-husband. When Garrett would say I was being foolish or thinking like a woman instead of someone rational. Once again, I wondered why I'd stayed with him as long as I had. Maybe that memory brought the answer to my mind. "Well, there you go. If Nick was the one who slipped bananas into Sally Apple's apple butter, you said it yourself—he served it to her. Why would he put banana in *three* of the jars? Seems a little overkill, doesn't it?"

"Because..." Branson paused again, and I heard an intake of breath, and then a little chuckle. "You know, that's a good question."

"Of course it is." I couldn't help myself.

He laughed, that time for real. "So sure of yourself, aren't you?" He didn't wait for a reply. "I really love that about you."

And any comparison to my ex-husband faded away. As did any ability to figure out what to say next.

Branson saved me from that particular issue. "Any other loopholes in my theory you can see? And I really do want to know."

I could tell by his tone that he did. And I appreciated it. "No, not at the moment, but I'll keep thinking." I so wished I had a different answer to that.

"Please do. I want to make sure we have the right person to pay for these murders, not just a scapegoat."

"Then... you'll let Nick go?"

There was a long pause. "No. Not yet. Let me think about it. I'm not going to move too fast. I want to do this correctly. No matter which way it goes. Even with that question, we have more than enough evidence that points directly at Nick, and motive. And not just with Sally Apple. From both Carla and Tiffany's testimonies, it sounds like Eustace Beaker said pretty derogatory things to that kid on a regular basis. Not surprising considering Eustace, but maybe more than a high school senior can manage and deal with. Even so, doesn't mean murder is the right way to go."

I couldn't argue with his logic. Even if my gut still screamed that Nick didn't do it. I scrambled to think of some other argument, some other thing that would poke a sizable hole into the evidence pointing at Nick, but I couldn't.

"Fred?"

The hesitant tone of Branson's voice both surprised me and brought me out of my head. "Yeah?"

"Don't let this hurt where we're headed, okay? I'm not shutting you out. I'm not ignoring you. I'm not insulting your intelligence or your ability. But where we are with the case, right now, this is where everything points. I can't very well use 'Winifred Page's gut said the kid didn't do it and I'm going to listen to her' as a legitimate reason to drop the charges against Nick." He rushed ahead before I could respond. "I will say this. You've made me wonder, and I'll keep looking at other angles. I would've anyway, but I'll do so even more now. That's gotta be good enough. Don't hold it against me for doing my job."

Where were we headed? A surge of anxiety rocketed through me at that thought.

"Fred?"

There was that almost-beseeching tone again. "I won't. I know how police work goes, remember? I won't hold it against you."

FIFTEEN

By the time I locked up the Cozy Corgi, I felt spent, both physically and emotionally. The morning had been devoted to my concerns over Nick, trying to determine exactly why I felt so strongly he was innocent. Branson was right; he did have motive. Plenty. He also had opportunity in spades. But yet, I couldn't see him doing it.

Every time that thought ran through my head, I couldn't help but chide myself. I hadn't bothered to learn the kid's name until a few days before, yet there I was emphatic that the police had taken in the wrong person. What was that about?

And even that, the waffling back and forth and questioning of my gut feelings, where was that coming from? If anything, I should trust my gut more than ever after the last several months.

Something about this situation was throwing me off, making me doubt my instincts. I thought it was

Carla, or my guilt around her, well-placed or not. When I moved to Estes, there wasn't a bookshop in town. I wasn't going into competition with anyone or having to worry about whether my choices would impact their livelihood. Even then, Carla and I hadn't been very chummy, but once Katie opened her bakery, things truly went south. And I couldn't blame Carla. Estes was a small town. And sure, the summer months were flush with tourists and cash, but most businesses had to hoard that cash to make it through the winter. Not only was the Cozy Corgi now a very real competition for Carla, but I was sticking my nose into the death of her father-in-law.

Or... maybe... my possible relationship with Branson was throwing me off.

I turned the key in the deadbolt and glared at the door handle like it was at fault, then looked down at Watson, who was staring at me with that expression that said, *Mom's being weird again.* He wasn't wrong. How long had I been standing there lost in my thoughts?

"You know what, Watson? Enough. I'm beating myself up for no reason. There's been a world of change over the past few months, and just as many dead bodies. A person is allowed to take some time to adjust."

Watson offered neither commentary nor insight, only chuffed and pulled at his leash.

"Fine. You raise a good point. Too much over-thinking and introspection will drive us insane. Let's go home."

We'd barely taken two steps when I glanced across the street and saw Carl and Anna both staring at us from the windows of Cabin and Hearth. They'd probably been watching me standing trans-fixed at the door the entire time. They both waved, unconcerned about being caught staring, and I waved back. They turned and disappeared into the shop.

I paused for a moment, Watson once more straining on his leash, ready to go. Carl and Anna weren't necessarily a bad idea. Even if they hadn't heard the rumors the high school kids spread about Nick, it sounded like there was also plenty of gossip about his family. Maybe that would offer some insight.

There I went again, not trusting my gut. If I didn't think it was Nick, then why would I need to get into whatever drama his family might be involved in?

Unless he was the one being set up, not Carla.

Even as I rejected speaking to the Hansons, my gaze wandered over to Paws.

There. That's where I should go. The possibility of the town council being the target seemed like a legitimate option, and Paulie had enough negative interactions with the group of them that he might have a lead he didn't even realize he possessed.

I glanced both ways along the street, lucked out with a large gap between traffic, and hurried across with Watson by my side. "You're going to hate me for this. But I bet you'll get a treat out of it."

Even as we sprinted across, he gave a little hop at his most beloved word, but his cheerful expression fell as we neared the front door of the pet shop and he cast accusatory brown eyes up at me.

"I know, I warned you. You're going to hate me." I pointed my finger down at him. "Behave, be nice. If you have to bite one of them, at least do it where Paulie doesn't see." Right, because giving Watson directives always worked.

The door had barely closed behind us when barking chaos erupted from somewhere in the back. Watson instantly slunk behind my legs.

Like warring tumbleweeds, Flotsam and Jetsam stampeded from one of the aisles and barreled our way.

Proving just how much I loved my little man, and how guilty I felt for putting him through another interaction with the two corgis, I knelt to the floor just in time to intercept the dogs, and was nearly bowled over by the impact of puppy paws, tongues, and friendly nips.

Even though he'd been spared, for the moment, Watson gave a warning growl.

"Whoa! I could barely see behind the tornado of dog hair!" Paulie emerged the way of his corgis, and the beaming expression on his face matched Flotsam and Jetsam's enthusiasm. "Talk about my lucky week. Nice to see you again so soon."

He hadn't been kidding about the dog hair. Every once in a while, I played with the idea of getting a brother or sister for Watson, even though I knew he was just an excuse. *I* would be the one wanting a second dog. Watson would be irritated that he was no longer king of the castle. But my life was already filled with too much corgi hair the way it was; this was a good reminder.

Mentally apologizing to Watson, I managed to extricate myself from Flotsam and Jetsam's affections and stood, trying to clear the dog hair away from my eyes.

Watson darted under my skirt, which created an even more enjoyable scenario for Paulie's corgis.

Just when I thought I was on the verge of a wardrobe malfunction, Paulie clapped his hands loudly. "Boys! Treats!"

Flotsam and Jetsam rocketed away as Paulie hurried behind the counter and got some large green dog bones from a bin.

Watson peered out from underneath my skirt, clearly debating if he valued his love of food or hermit status more. Paulie waved one of the green bones in his direction. "Got one for you too, Watson!" And the decision was made.

The bones were substantial, and I hoped Flotsam and Jetsam would be distracted for long enough that by the time they were finished, the novelty of Watson's presence would've worn off.

"Sorry about that, Fred. My boys are a little enthusiastic, as you know." He sighed and leaned against the counter. "What brings you in? I know you said Watson isn't doing the dog food." His tone grew wary. "More questions about Athena?"

"No. Not exactly. I was hoping to get some specifics about your experiences with the town council."

"Sure. Anything I can do to help." He sounded relieved and sighed again.

Actually, as I crossed the space, with the bubbling and hum of fish tanks in the back and the chirping of birds from the cages surrounding us, I realized he seemed a little more than relieved. He looked exhausted, even thinner than normal, with dark circles under his eyes. I hadn't noticed him being so worn out when I'd seen him at Aspen Grove. I placed my hand over his as I reached him and was pleasantly surprised to find that I felt genuine concern. Like I would for a friend. Maybe we'd finally crossed that line. Genuinely. "Are you okay? You look tired."

Paulie stared down at our hands, blinked rapidly, and sniffed. When he met my gaze, there was a sheen in his eyes, but the smile he gave lessened his apparent exhaustion. "I'm okay. Thank you for asking."

I patted his hand before releasing it. "Are you sure? You don't have to be okay."

He was close to tears, but he straightened, and though his tone didn't harden, I saw a wall go up behind his eyes I hadn't seen before. "I do appreciate it. But I'm okay, or I will be." Even with the wall, his smile was sincere. "You mentioned the town council?

Anything specific, or do you just want me to give an exhaustive list of grievances I have with them?"

I was a little surprised about how concerned I truly was about Paulie. Clearly, something was wrong, but part of friendship was giving space and not pressuring. "Well, if you're sure you're up for it, whatever you want to share would be great. I know you said when you moved to town they gave you a hard time around opening your business. That you felt it was because you weren't a local."

He nodded. "Yeah. From what I've heard, that's not too unusual for a lot of the businesses moving to town." He shrugged his thin shoulders. "Although it does seem to matter what type of business it is and who the new person is. If they measure up to the standard."

"What standard?"

Another shrug. He seemed to struggle to find words and then shrugged again. "For lack of a better term, Fred, it's basically the cool factor. High school all over again. You're either one of the cool kids or you're not. I never was. I never will be." He smiled sadly but sounded resigned. "I'm okay with that. Although I will say, it's a little more frustrating when trying to operate a business than it was in high school. And every bit as lonely. But I'm one of the lucky ones. Sergeant Wexler helped clear the way for me. Not everyone has that. And even with him, the council balked."

Paulie had said enough in the past that it was clear he and Branson had a mixed history. They obviously didn't like each other, yet from time to time there were comments like that—where it seemed Paulie felt he owed Branson.

"Sergeant Wexler went to bat for you when he doesn't others?"

Again Paulie struggled for words. "I know you and Branson have a relationship. I want to help you however I can, but I'd rather keep Branson out of it, if you don't mind."

"Sure. No pressure to tell me anything you're not comfortable with." I didn't feel like it had anything to do with what was going on with Carla, but there was definitely something there. And whether Paulie and I had an actual friendship or not, I wanted to know what it was.

Before I could figure out how to start again, there were several loud yips, a clattering of claws, and a loud metallic clang, followed by the screeching of a parrot.

"Flotsam! Jetsam! Come!" Paulie clapped his hands again.

Though they didn't obey his command, there was another yip, and things quieted down.

Watson arrived at my feet from the opposite direction, so at least he hadn't been involved in whatever occurred. He slunk under my skirt once more, and I felt him curl up, resting his head on my boot.

Paulie refocused on me. "Where would you like me to start?"

It was a good question. I had no answer.

Friendship being new or not, I trusted Paulie. Had ever since he helped when Watson had been hurt around Christmas. He also had never given me any indication that he took part in the gossip. Granted, with his limited social engagement, that probably wasn't much of an option for him. I decided to take him into my confidence. "I'm wondering if Eustace's and Sally's deaths might indicate a larger pattern. Since they were both part of the town council. With a group that, like you've said, have made it miserable for a lot of new people in town—and some old ones from what I've heard—that maybe someone thought it was time for a change in power."

His bloodshot eyes widened, and there was a flash of interest. "You think somebody might be working their way through the town council?"

"I don't know. It's just a theory."

"I heard they arrested one of Carla's baristas." There was another commotion in the back, followed by a bark. He paused, but when it quieted down, he refocused on me. "You're not convinced."

"No. I'm not. I'm not saying it's definitely about the town council either, but maybe. Sounds like they've made a lot of enemies."

"They aren't all bad, so I hope you're wrong. Elmer Walton, the guy who operates Chipmunk Mountain, really took me under his wing when I got into town. It just seems like the louder voices on that council are the meanest." He leaned a little closer, his voice lowering as if Flotsam and Jetsam or the birds, fish, and array of rodents might overhear. "If they are going through the town council, they're going to have to start over. Ethel has already taken Eustace's place."

Maybe Paulie was a little more involved in the gossip around town than I thought. It took me a second to place Ethel's name, but when I did, it gave me a little jolt. "Eustace's wife? She just slid in and took his spot?"

He nodded.

"Aren't those elected positions? Surely she can't just decide to take it over."

"Pretty sure she can. At least the way it seems

like the town council works. Maybe there's a loop-hole if someone dies in between election cycles."

That seemed revolting. "Someone should contact a lawyer. From what you said, it sounds like Gerald Jackson isn't afraid to take them on." I couldn't believe those words had just come out of my mouth. He was the worst excuse for a lawyer I'd ever seen.

Paulie scoffed and rolled his eyes. "Gerald does what he can, but Sally's husband, Colin, is a lawyer too. Gerald was able to help Athena in her fight with Eustace, but if it hadn't been for Colin, she would've gotten her job back. I'm sure Sally's husband has made certain every I is dotted and every T is crossed with Ethel replacing Eustace on the council."

"Sally Apple was married to a lawyer?"

"Yeah." He nodded. "Colin Apple."

"And he's part of the reason Athena didn't get her position back as restaurant reviewer at the paper, even though she clearly had legal standing to fight Eustace?"

"Yes. It's only thanks to Gerald that she got what she has now. In fact—" His words broke off, and this time when the wall shot back up behind his eyes, there was a coldness to him.

Clearly, he'd realized where my mind had already gone.

"Fred, I know how that sounded. You can't think that. Athena is wonderful. She would never hurt anyone."

The cards were stacking against her, though. The first victim was the one who had taken away her dream job and probably lorded it over her as much as he could at work, and the second was one who'd discriminated against her granddaughter and was married to a lawyer who was part of her not being allowed to live her passion. A lawyer who more than likely protected his wife when complaints were made about her treatment of students.

Maybe this had nothing to do with the town council after all, just two of its more insidious members.

And... maybe...Colin Apple was about to get a poisonous scone of his own.

"Fred." Paulie's sharp tone brought me back to the moment. "It's not Athena. It isn't."

I didn't want it to be, either. I agreed with Katie. I liked her. In many ways I admired her. I tried to get a read on my gut, my instinct about her, but couldn't either way.

"Fred. It really *isn't* Athena. She's an amazing woman and a wonderful friend. She'd never hurt anyone." Paulie muttered a little curse and seemed close to tears again, though these were different than the first. "Me and my big mouth. I just said it wrong. I'm making it sound worse than what it is." He shook his head. "No more. I just keep making it worse and worse." He leveled his stare at me, and even before he spoke, I could see that the words cost him. "I think you need to go, Fred. Sorry. But... please leave."

SIXTEEN

Athena swiveled in her chair and smiled as I knocked on her office door at *The Chipmunk Chronicles*. As the other times I'd seen her, she was magazine-cover perfect. Makeup flawless, she somehow made a startling pink-and-yellow suit look timeless and elegant. If I would've attempted such an outfit, people would've thought it was Halloween. "Winifred Page and Watson. I must admit, when the receptionist said you were here, I was surprised. I wasn't expecting you until this afternoon." She bent forward slightly and offered an outstretched hand to Watson.

He entered the office, touched his nose to her skin, and allowed himself to be stroked.

"I suppose Paulie called you last night?" I'd anticipated as much.

She straightened and smoothed out her already smooth skirt. "That he did. The poor boy was a mess, thinking he'd implicated me in unseemly activities." She actually grinned as she gestured toward the seat I'd occupied before. "Come on in, Fred. No need to play games. We both know why you're here."

I followed her directive. Though I'd figured Paulie had given her a warning call, I hadn't been certain of what sort of welcome I might get when I dropped in. I handed her a small paper box with the Cozy Corgi logo on the top. I'd had Katie prepare an assortment. "Just in case you haven't had breakfast."

She lifted one of her perfectly sculpted brows. "Bribery?" She lifted the lid, took a deep breath, and sighed. "I accept. That business partner of yours knows what she's doing."

"Yes, she does." I wasn't sure how to respond to the bribery comments so I jumped over it.

"She can say the same. You know what you're doing too, Fred." Athena shut the pastry box and placed it on the other side of her desk. "Let's get to it. Are you going with questioning or accusation?"

I'd been wondering the same. "As you said, you know why I'm here, so why don't you tell me."

Her cranberry smile grew, and she glanced at Watson. "Does your mama always play such games?"

Watson cocked his head quizzically in her direction.

Chuckling, she looked back at me. "You suspect me of killing people, Fred. I'm hardly going to make it easy for you. It's a rather insulting thought, don't you agree? You might as well have the audacity to come out and say it."

"I don't know what I think, to be honest." I appreciated she was the kind to not play games, to go with the straightforward approach. However, maybe the straightforward approach was, in and of itself, a game. I didn't think I had another option than playing along. "I like you. For several reasons, some I can't quite label. But one of them is that you seem strong, determined—maybe part of that is enacting revenge when you've been wronged. Obviously, I don't know you well, but you don't seem to be the type to allow yourself to be told what to do." I gestured around the small office. "But here you are, writing obituaries."

"You've got my number there, honey. And don't you forget it. No one tells Athena Rose what she can or can't do." She paused, eyes sparkling in a way that confirmed we were playing a game after all. "But in case you haven't noticed, Eustace Beaker has been dead for more than a hot minute, and I'm still here writing obituaries. If I killed him to get my old job back, why would I still be here?"

"Because it was never about you. Maybe it was never about power plays, punishments, or obituaries." If Athena had killed Eustace and Sally, I was certain I was right about *the why*. "And while I do believe that no one tells you what to do, I bet that's doubly so for your granddaughter." No, I wasn't sure if she'd killed, but I could see her doing it. Even at her age and delicate stature, the woman radiated power.

Her eyes widened, ever so slightly, revealing that she hadn't expected that. "You are good at snooping, aren't you? And I mean that as a compliment. Truly. You would make one bang-up reporter." She let out a long breath, and her gaze hardened somewhat. "Let me tell you something about my granddaughter. Odessa is *not* a victim. Did we lose a battle about that stupid valedictorian garbage? Yes. Though it burns me to admit, we did. But I'm thankful for it." She leaned forward slightly and tapped the desk with a french-tipped nail. "She was already a fighter, just like her grandmother, but that event made it even more true. She would've been successful either way, but that lit a fire under her. Now if you flew your sweet little butt to New York City this afternoon, you'd have to pay one hundred and fifty dollars to sit in a seat just to watch her sing and perform.

And she's not some backup, not part of some ensemble cast, no ma'am." She shook her head and gave a little hum of pride. "She's the star of the whole show."

We stared at each other, and she communicated just as strongly in the silence as she had with words. We might be playing a game together, she and I, but there was no playing around with Athena Rose.

She tapped the desk again, nodded, and sat back. "I'll tell you just as plain as I did the other day. I won't shed a tear that Sally Apple is no longer with us. Just like with Eustace, the world's better off without them. But just like so many horrible things in life, I'm thankful for them. They made us stronger. They applied the pressure to turn coal into diamonds. And we shine, Odessa and I. We shine."

I had no argument there. Neither could I find any words.

Her phone beeped on her desk, and Athena continued her measuring gaze of me for several more moments, allowing it to beep a few more times before finally turning away and lifting the receiver. "Yes?"

There was a blurred voice on the other end of the line.

"You've got to be kidding me?" Athena gave a sigh and shook her head in irritation. "Goodness no.

Don't send her back. I'll be right up." She ended the call and stood. "Excuse me, Fred. Ms. Jessup's father passed six months ago. And yet she's still complaining about the obituary." Her smile returned to a smirk. "Now, I ask you, how is it my fault that he had a second secret family in Allenspark and I just happened to list his other set of descendants while I was documenting his life?"

Despite myself, I chuckled. Yes, I did like her. "Watson and I can step out if you need to talk to her in your office."

"You're not done with me yet, I see." She nodded in what looked like approval. "No, stay. I actually appreciate it. It gives me a legitimate excuse to only listen to a couple of minutes of her complaints. I'll be right back." She stepped out of the office and then swiveled once more. "There're some lovely pastries in the box on my desk; help yourself." And with a wink, she was gone.

Even if my admiration was growing for Athena, I didn't feel like I had a good read on her. I wasn't sure if she'd had anything to do with the recent deaths, but something about her made me certain she was capable of murder, if she needed to be. But I thought that was true with most strong people.

I was glad for the interruption. It gave me a

chance to try to clear my head and figure out what direction to go. Maybe I was wasting my time talking to Athena. And though my instincts didn't tell me if she'd killed Eustace or Sally, they said there was more to the woman than she was letting on. But again, I thought that was true with most people.

A huffing sound caught my attention, and I looked over to see Watson had managed to prop himself up on the partially open drawer and was using his nose to shove the box of pastries closer to the edge of the desk.

"Watson!"

At my startled admonition, Watson jerked and not only succeeded in knocking off the pastries but a pile of notebooks and papers as well. Knowing he was in trouble, he ducked his head and slunk toward me. He gave me those big brown puppy eyes that begged for forgiveness. Before I could decide to grant it or not, his gaze darted toward the partially open box on the floor.

"Oh no you don't, you little scamp." I got up from my chair and scooped the box from the floor. Though dented, it seemed the pastries weren't all that much the worse for wear.

Watson took shelter under the chair I'd been

sitting in as I scooped up the papers and managed to make some semblance of a pile on Athena's desk.

Just as I was about to walk back to the chair, Sally Apple's name caught my attention from the top piece of paper.

With a glance out the office door to confirm Athena wasn't on her way back, I lifted it and began to read. Athena's handwritten script was as elegant as I would've expected. It nearly resembled calligraphy.

The first part was like any other obituary, listing dates and family and career. I couldn't imagine what it would be like to write the obituaries of people you despised. Did Athena revel in it? Have a sense of retribution finally coming to roost? Or did she battle with the desire to say what she really thought about the person?

From the looks of it, it seemed Athena was the ultimate professional. I never would've guessed her true feelings about Sally Apple. Until the closing line, at any rate.

Sally Apple was a woman with subpellucid patrician sensibilities and lived her life accordingly.

I had to read the sentence three times to make sense of it. It sounded fancy; it sounded like a compliment. And maybe, if I didn't know Athena, I would continue to read it as such.

But it wasn't.

Patrician, like an aristocrat. Complimentary in one way, but really, it denoted someone who saw themselves above everyone else. The top of a hierarchy. And that did seem to sum up what I'd witnessed about Sally.

I started to set the paper back on the desk, then paused. Something else bugged me about the phrasing.

Subpellucid patrician sensibilities. Really, it was nothing more than an insult closed in fancy verbiage. Sally Apple clearly had arrogant and elitist sensibilities. Obvious. And true.

I read it again. There was something else. Something nagging at me, shouting that it was right in front of my face if I would just open my eyes.

"I didn't know by offering your pastries that I gave you an invitation to read things on my desk? Even if you were the one to bring in the pastries to begin with."

I jumped at Athena's voice, and whipped around to find her studying me from the doorway.

She was more amused than offended. "I'm afraid I have to deduct points, Fred. You're not as good at snooping as I thought if you get caught so easily." She entered the small office, and we did a bit of a dance so she could retake her seat.

As I sat back down in mine, which still housed the sulking Watson underneath, I held the paper out toward her. "Sally's obituary. Sorry. Watson tried to help himself to breakfast and knocked things off your desk. I couldn't help myself."

She didn't take it. "The younger ones here make fun of me. I have to write out everything before I put it into the computer." She folded her hands in her lap. "Tell me, did you find proof of me murdering Sally in what I'd written?"

I withdrew the paper and studied her. "You know, I won't disagree with you. Eustace and Sally seemed like miserable people, but *you* seem to be finding their deaths a little more of a game than I'm comfortable with."

She didn't even flinch. "I'm not the one pretending to be a detective, Winifred. Some would say you're the one playing the game. Even if you are good at it. And... I'm not concerned whether you're comfortable with my attitude toward Eustace's and Sally's deaths."

"And what about Nick Pacheco? I'm sure you've

heard he's under arrest. Is an innocent teenager taking the fall a game as well?"

She winced. "No. Most definitely not. I don't know the boy, though I know *of* him. Of his family. From what little I've observed, I don't see him as being capable of murder. But no, if he is innocent, then it most definitely is not a game."

Suddenly I was tired of it. And I felt like I was wasting my time. I didn't think Athena had killed them, even if she was glad they were dead. "I'll quit wasting your time. Watson and I will..." I'd started to slide the obituary back on her desk, but once more, the last line caught my eye. More specifically, one word caught my eye, and I gasped.

Subpellucid.

And it clicked.

"Pellucid."

I hadn't meant to say the word out loud, but I looked up at Athena, and for the first time since I'd known her, she tensed.

Pellucid.

"You're Maxine Maxwell, aren't you? You write the Sybarite blog."

She stiffened, and I saw the denial rise to her lips, but then she closed her mouth and seemed to deflate somewhat in her chair. The flash of weakness was only for a moment. Less than. She straightened once more, defiantly lifting her chin. "I told you. No one tells me what I can or cannot do."

And with that, I was certain. Maybe that's why I hadn't been able to have a genuine gut feeling about her. I'd sensed a secret, just not the one I'd been searching for. I laid the paper back on her desk. "I'm assuming there'd be litigation, due to the terms of your agreement with Eustace Beaker in the paper, if it was discovered you're doing a food blog."

"There would." She nodded primly. "Although, I'm talking to my lawyer since Eustace's death and seeing if there's a loophole to change that particular situation."

Her lawyer, Gerald Jackson. I hoped he was better than I thought he was, for Athena's sake.

"You didn't kill Eustace or Sally, did you?"

"I told you as much."

True. She had. I felt a strange sense of relief in finally believing her. And a little justification of having liked her on such an instant level. But it meant I was back to square one. Still, I was relieved.

Athena leaned forward once more, and though the defiance didn't leave her gaze, there was the slightest quaver in her words. "I trust I can count on your discretion until I have this matter sorted?"

"Absolutely." Any other option wasn't even a thought. I smiled over at her, suddenly liking her even more than I had previously. "I have to thank you. Having such a beautiful review in the Sybarite blog might've been the highlight of Katie's entire life."

"Well..." She smiled, and Athena Rose was fully herself once again. "Just shows she has superb taste."

SEVENTEEN

"I think our husbands paid Harold to drive Carla's car through our shop." Zelda stood, hands on her hips, and glared at the inside of Lois's old candy store, Healthy Delights. "They get to go to a conference, and we have to work on their shop."

Verona crossed the room and nudged her twin playfully with her hip. "Interesting theory, but I'd rather be here than at a conference filled with inventors. I can barely keep my eyes from glazing over when Jonah and Noah get going. Can you imagine hundreds of them all together?"

They shuddered as one at the thought. Barry's daughters were identical. Just slightly shorter than me, but willowy and graceful. They both dressed in Barry's style of yoga garb, but theirs were always from natural fibers and never clashed like Barry's color combos often did. The only visible difference was Verona's blonde hair compared to Zelda's brunette.

Barry joined them, Watson prancing around his feet, and threw his arms over their shoulders. "Don't be ungrateful, girls. Remember, thanks to Harold's adventure, you get to redesign the front of your shop. That's worth it, right?"

"Now that's just awful!" Mom peered out from the display case she'd been inspecting. "That was hardly an adventure. Poor Harold was in the middle of one of his seizures. And Percival and Gary could've been killed." She held up a small cellophane-wrapped brown ball. "I think I found some of Lois's licorice candy in here. Do you think it's still good?"

"Probably. The only good thing that poor woman ever could make."

"Dad." Verona swatted at Barry as she ducked from under his arm, sounding more like a teenager than a woman in her forties. "She was on a mission to make the world healthier. Sugar kills more people than guns."

Though Zelda nodded along, I knew it was for show. I'd caught her at the ice cream parlor a few weeks before, and she swore me to secrecy. The twins were proud of living their all-natural, organic lifestyle. Turned out, only one of them actually was.

We'd only been in the shop a matter of minutes, and I leaned against the wall, letting their bickering fade to a pleasant background buzz. After striking Athena off my suspect list that morning, I was a bit exhausted between the onslaught of tourists at the bookshop while replaying different scenarios through my mind.

I was back to thinking it had to be about taking vengeance on the city council. But who in their right mind thought they could successfully murder all six members? And if the council was going to just simply replace members as Ethel had done with her husband, the murders would never stop. It didn't add up.

Though I hated to admit it, picturing Nick being the one who was responsible made more sense. It made perfect sense, actually, when put down in black-and-white, which was exactly what I'd done in between customers during the day. The only reason it didn't work, was my gut feeling that he simply couldn't do it. Maybe I was wrong. As much as I hated to think about him being capable of such actions, it would mean that everyone else was safe.

There were no more poison scones or anything else headed in anyone's direction.

"You having a hard time in here, darling?" Mom arrived, smoothing her small hand over my back. She smiled up at me in concern. "The girls and Barry won't mind if you don't help. I know this place has bad memories for you."

"What?" I'd been so caught up in my thoughts I hadn't noticed her come over, and it took me a few seconds to interpret her meaning. "Oh, no. I wasn't even thinking about what happened in here."

Though now that she mentioned it, I supposed it was strange it hadn't hit me before. It had been months since I'd been in the all-natural candy shop, with its walls and counters painted sickeningly sweet pastel pinks and yellows. Despite myself, I glanced toward the door that led to the back room. My time in Estes had nearly been so short. I shook it off. That was in the past; we were a long way from that. I never would've envisioned trying to get the store ready for my brothers-in-law the first time I'd walked into Healthy Delights.

I refocused on Mom "I really am fine. Truly. I was just thinking about Nick, the barista at Carla's coffee shop."

Mom nodded. "Yes. I heard he's been arrested. Breaks my heart for someone so young." Her eyes glistened with emotion, but she straightened her small frame. She still had the core of strength every spouse of a police officer had to have. "You just never know, do you?"

"I suppose not."

"Though it sounds horrible to say, there is one plus side." Mom glanced over as Barry guffawed at something the twins said, then back at me. "I visited Harold this morning. He seems better. Oh, he was so terrified about what all this was going to do to Carla and the business. I know Nick was connected to the coffee shop, and Carla, obviously, but at least it takes the suspicion off her and allows Black Bear Roaster to reopen soon. That's going to do Harold a world of good to be able to alleviate that stress."

"That's one way to look at it." I was going to need to find *some* bright side to all of this.

Her blue eyes narrowed, knowingly. "You think the police are wrong."

Did I? Even still? "I think so. I really do. But every other possibility I come up with either is proven untrue or simply is too farfetched to make sense."

She inspected me a little longer and then sighed in resignation. "Well, then I'm sure you'll figure it out. Quickly, I hope. For Harold's sake, if nothing else. He had another seizure while I was there today, just a few moments. Honestly, I probably wouldn't have noticed that if not for the other day, but still."

"Mom..." Her belief in me never ceased to amaze me. "Just because I think the police are wrong doesn't mean that they are."

She didn't hesitate. "I know that look, Fred. It's the same one your father would get toward the end of the case, especially when everyone thought it was nearly wrapped up but something wasn't sitting right with him. He'd get that same expression in his eyes, and that same tone of voice. And he was never wrong. Not once."

"Not once?" The skepticism in my voice surprised me and gave a little spike of guilt that I would doubt my father, who was enshrined to hero status in my mind.

"No. Not once." Mom tilted her chin. "To be honest, he doubted himself a lot. He would get a gut feeling—that's what he'd call it, a gut feeling—and wouldn't be able to shake it off. All the facts would be pointing one way, and he wouldn't buy them. He spent many nights worrying about them. Telling me how silly he felt for believing a certain way when the facts pointed a different direction. He was never wrong. And it always hurts a little how much he distrusted himself."

I gaped at her, and my skin tingled with goose-flesh. "Did he really?"

"He did." She nodded, and a look of longing and love settled over her features. "I didn't trust his gut feelings at first either. But after a couple of years, they'd been proven true often enough that I never doubted. Even when he did. As soon as he started that little cycle of worrying and questioning all that was happening simply because he felt differently, I always knew how it would end."

I could almost feel him with us right there, even with Barry and the twins—the evidence of life continuing and moving in new and unexpected ways —just a few feet from us. "I'm sure it helped a lot having a wife like you, someone who always believed in him."

"Oh, Fred, darling." She lifted her birdlike hand and cupped my face. "Your dad was lucky—he had me, *and* he had you."

My eyes stung.

She continued. "You are luckier. You have a host of people who believe in you completely. Me, always. Barry, obviously. Katie, Leo." She grinned playfully and cast a glance over at the group of four across the shop and then back at me. "And Watson, of course."

I chuckled and sniffed. "Thanks, Mom." It felt like more words were needed, but I couldn't find them. And even if I did, I wouldn't be able to say them without giving in to the emotions.

She simply smiled, and I could see she knew all that I couldn't say. "Let it go for a little bit. You'll figure it out. You're just like your dad, and he always thought best when he was working on something else. Let's go help the family." She slipped her hand into mine, and we left the little sacred place.

"Noah wants to name this place Synapses." Zelda cast a wide-eyed glance at Mom and me as we joined the circle. "*Synapses*! Because *that's* not going to alienate people from coming in, lording it over how they are smarter than everyone else."

Verona gave a matching expression. "It's better than what Jonah wants. Inventors-R-Us sounds like a toyshop for honor roll students."

Another wave of emotions washed over me at the conversation. A little tingle of fear. It seemed unreal that Katie and I would soon be flanked by my twin stepsisters' new age shop on one side and their husbands' inventor store on the other. But it was happening. It was really happening. Fear was probably too strong a word for it; maybe just a sense of wonder or surprise was more appropriate.

"Are you girls still thinking you're going to name your shop Chakras?" Barry looked up from where he was lavishing attention on Watson, who was nearly comatose in pleasure. He was clearly trying to distract and avoid a tangent.

"Oh, absolutely." Verona nodded in excitement, getting swept up in Barry's ploy.

"In fact..." Zelda matched her sister's tone and glanced at me. "We're going to use the same company that created your sign for the Cozy Corgi. Though ours will be made out of wood as well, we're thinking a yellow-and-green tie-dyed background with the word Chakras in gold lettering."

No, no... fear was the right word. Fear and dread, with a little wave of nausea thrown in. "Well... that sounds... just..."

Mom squeezed my hand. "Lovely. Very soothing."

Zelda beamed. "It's going to be wonderful. A little oasis of tranquility in the center of the downtown bustle."

I had to bite my lip to keep my smirk from

turning into a laugh. The downtown bustle. As if it was going to be on the chaotic streets of Kansas City's Plaza district.

Proving that I'd done a good job masking my reaction, Verona leaned in with lowered voice, even though there was no one else to overhear. "Zelda and I have massages scheduled at Pinecone Manor tomorrow. We're going to talk to some of the massage therapists and see if they'd be interested in a side gig at Chakras. We were thinking we might set up one of those little massage chairs in the backend and have guest massage therapists come in to offer tranquility sessions to our patrons."

"Oh, that sounds lovely. I haven't had a treatment at Pinecone Manor since I moved back here," Mom chimed in, ever graceful.

As one, the twins each reached for one of Mom's hands. "Come with us. We'll treat you to a full half-day experience. It's the least we can do for all the help you've been."

Sometimes Verona and Zelda were a little too much for me, especially combined with their husbands and children. It all took some getting used to, but moments like these, when they were so kind to my mother, made up for a world of idiosyncrasies.

"Make sure you let them know you're my daughters. I'm sure you'll get a discount." Barry finished rubbing Watson's belly and stood, eliciting a heartbroken stare from my little man that Barry didn't notice. "But don't mention you're trying to steal their employees."

My hippie-dippie stepfather. It still baffled me how he seemed to have a touch point for every place in Estes. Even at one of the most exclusive bed-and-breakfast and spas in Estes. "Don't tell me you own Pinecone Manor, too?"

He grinned at me and shrugged. "I did, sort of."

Mom sucked in a gasp. "Oh, right. I'd forgotten. You all bought that property your senior year in high school. You closed on it right after graduation."

Barry slipped his arm over Mom's shoulder and pulled her close. "Good memory, my dear." He waggled his eyebrows at Verona, Zelda, and me. "It was the first property I ever bought. An act of rebellion more than anything, trying to prove to my parents that I could make my own way." He chuckled. "Though considering there were five of us, I suppose that hardly proved anything."

"You bought your first property before you even graduated high school?"

He nodded. "Pretty much. It was just an empty stretch of land back then. Beautiful, but completely undeveloped, and nothing around it at all. The man who owned it—" He snapped his fingers as he tried to recall. "—Mr. Bruce something." More snapping. "No, Bruce was his last name. Mr. Something Bruce." He shook his head. "It doesn't matter, beside the point. Either way, Mr. Bruce died, and his wife decided to sell everything and move back east. Sold her house and a few different pieces of property they owned. That particular lot was the farthest out of town and the cheapest."

"You talking about Pinecone Manor?" I hadn't noticed the door opening, but Percival and Gary walked in, late as normal. Percival limped and held Gary's hand for support as they shut the door and walked toward us. Though he clearly was hurting, he grinned at Barry. "Still kicking yourself for selling too early?"

"I've done all right—in case you haven't noticed." Barry winked, and there was a quick round of hugs in way of greeting.

Mom rubbed Percival's arm. "You look worse today."

He shrugged. "Well, baby sister, we're not as young as we used to be. Granted, I've never almost been run over by a car before, but for being a man in my seventies, I think I'm managing pretty well."

"You should see him in the mornings, he's as stiff as a scarecrow nailed to a cross." Gary cast a loving, yet exasperated, eye roll toward Percival. "And he won't even use any pain-reliever ointment to help loosen him up."

Percival let out a shocked gasp and swatted at Gary. "Dear Lord, quit bringing that up. Just because I've turned into an old man doesn't mean I have to smell like one!" He noticed Watson at Barry's feet and started to bend down with a flourish. "Well, hello there, little—" His words broke off with a sharp intake of breath at the exact moment Watson darted away. Percival attempted to straighten with a wince and narrowed his eyes at me. "Moved a little too quickly there. I swear that dog of yours hates me."

"Well, I'm sure lurching at him like a zombie makes him feel perfectly safe and secure." Though Gary sniped at him, he assisted Percival in standing upright.

Barry sank to one knee and offered Watson all the comfort he could desire before focusing on Percival. "Yes, I was talking about Pinecone Manor. And, no, I'm just fine how the whole thing turned out."

Percival chuckled happily. "Me too, believe me. Gary's and my little antique store wouldn't exist otherwise."

I latched on to the topic. A family history lesson would help distract from thoughts of Nick that were fighting to come back in. "How in the world is Pinecone Manor associated with Victorian Antlers?"

"It's not, other than it helped pay for the place." Percival motioned toward Barry. "Go ahead, sounds like you are in midstory anyway. I'm fairly certain I have a rib out of place that makes even talking exhausting. Therefore, I defer to you, good sir."

Barry launched in again, just as it looked like Mom was about to begin a concerned lecture over Percival. "Well, like I was saying before, for all my desire for independence, I didn't have enough resources to buy the property outright, despite it being dirt cheap. So two of my classmates joined with me, and a couple of older guys who'd graduated a few years before"—he nodded toward Percival—"joined in."

"Sure, rub it in that I'm older." Percival scowled at Barry. "Although I've outlived Eustace, so I suppose that means I win."

"Percival, really!" Mom swatted at him gently, causing Percival to attempt to duck and wince once more.

"I suppose you're right, there." Barry chuckled.

Before Mom could scold him, Zelda surprised

me by voicing the question I was about to ask. "Eustace Beaker was the other guy who'd already graduated?"

Percival nodded. "Yep. And the only one of the lot of us who had more than a dime to his name. But still not enough to buy it on his own."

"Eustace more than made up for it in time, though, didn't he? Mr. Moneybags." As he spoke, Barry had a distant look in his eyes, as if he were far away. "Sally and Dolana and I were afraid once Eustace got involved that he was going to go behind our backs and buy our shares before closing. Still surprised he didn't."

"Sally?" Surely I was hearing wrong. "Sally Apple?"

"Yep." Barry turned to me, coming back to the present. "She, Dolana, and I all graduated together."

I hadn't placed that name the first time. "Dolana... Carla's grandmother?"

"Sure enough." He grinned over at Percival. "Of course that's what this one gives me a hard time about. Dolana and I both sold our shares within a couple of years. She was getting married and needed to pay for a dress and the wedding, and I found a store downtown I wanted to invest in." He pointed as if through the wall. "Your bookshop, actually, Fred."

"Worked out well for the rest of us. We made a fortune off that deal." Percival nodded along cheerfully.

"Took you long enough. You all had to sit on that land for thirty years before Clyde and Meisel bought it from you to build Pinecone Manor." Barry shrugged. "I used the rent I received from Fred's bookshop to help buy the next property. If I'd waited thirty years, I'd have nothing."

"Yes, I can't argue with you. You've done just fine." Percival also seemed lost to the past. "I asked Dolana about the property not long before she died, asked if she had any regrets about it. She didn't." He gave a soft, affectionate laugh. "She was a treasure, that one. Said it was the best decision she'd ever made. She took out that locket of hers that she always wore, showed the picture of her and Harold on their wedding day. Said she never would've been able to have such a beautiful dress if it hadn't been for selling her portion of that property. Even had enough for the down payment on the first house too."

I stared at Percival, then looked at Barry, then back again.

Maybe it was a gut feeling, maybe it was just common sense, maybe it was just one more factor of me being my father's daughter. Whatever it was, I knew the answer was in that story. Had to be. I felt it. Just as surely as I knew that Nick hadn't killed anyone.

A couple of hours later, Watson and I left the soon-to-be-renamed Healthy Delights. The family hadn't accomplished all that much. A little cleaning, but mostly we'd gotten lost to ordering pizza, one with vegan cheese for Barry, and simply enjoying one another's company.

Watson and I crossed in front of the Cozy Corgi on the way to the Mini Cooper. It wasn't until we were even with the plastic-covered hole in the side of Sinful Bites that it clicked. It was so obvious, I wondered how it hadn't hit me earlier, as soon as I'd heard Barry and Percival's story. Without waiting, I pulled out my cell, dialed Paulie, and asked for Athena's number. He took very little convincing, and then I called Athena.

She answered on the second ring. "This is Athena Rose." Even though it was pushing ten in the evening, she sounded like her ever cool and classic self.

"Hi, Athena, this is Fred. I have a favor to ask." For just a moment, I thought about reconsidering—

really thinking through it—then shoved it aside. There was no more pondering required. I was sure. "You think there's any chance you could write a review tonight and get it up on your Sybarite blog by morning?"

EIGHTEEN

Harold White glowered at Watson. Though, if I was reading him correctly, he was attempting to disguise his irritation that I'd brought my dog with me. The change in Harold was remarkable from the other time I'd visited with Barry. It looked like Mom had been right. Having Nick Pacheco in jail for the murders had put his fears for Carla at ease.

For his part, Watson didn't notice Harold's distaste for his presence. Then again, Watson had a general distaste for most people himself. Maybe he thought he'd found a kindred spirit. Either way, he curled up under the chair I'd sat in by the window and fell promptly asleep.

As Harold and I occupied the only two chairs in the room, Barry sat cross-legged on Harold's bed. He snacked away on one of Katie's chocolate chip scones, crumbs falling like snow over lime-green yoga pants and the bedspread. "Thanks for letting me have one of the pastries, Harold. I appreciate it."

"You're the one who brought them; technically they're yours." Harold cast another glower, this time at the Cozy Corgi box, then offered what seemed to be a genuine partial smile at Barry. "Besides, they just fed us breakfast less than fifteen minutes ago."

"Well, I'll make sure to only have one, leave the rest for you to..." Barry's gaze flicked to me, and I could read the guilt in his watery blue eyes. He cleared his throat and tried again. "I'll leave the rest for you to enjoy later."

Perhaps I should've felt guilty about having Katie box up an assortment of scones of all things. Should've felt guilty for what I'd asked Athena to do. Maybe even have a twinge of remorse for what I was getting ready to do to Harold, and by extension, Carla.

The Winifred Page of a few months ago would have. So much so, I doubted I'd been able to have pulled it off. Although, I hadn't done so yet, so I suppose that remained to be seen.

But I didn't. Not the slightest tingle of guilt, not for any of it. Save for one thing. When I'd moved to Estes Park half a year before, Barry was little more than my mother's husband. A man I liked but felt distant around, and a little apathetic toward. That was no longer the case. I positively adored the man. And what did he get for my love?

Me requesting things I knew cost him deeply, that's what.

He considered Harold a friend. But he knew I wouldn't be able to pull this off without him. Harold would be too much on guard if I were by myself.

Though I'd already known Barry adored me just as much as I did him, if I hadn't been clear on that fact, his willingness to take part in my plan, even though he wasn't convinced, proved it.

Maybe I could take a little pressure off him, or at least set the stage to ease him into it. I turned back to Harold. "You look a lot better than when we visited the other day. Brighter. Ms. Booger said your seizures have gotten less frequent." I'd already committed to lying my way through this gamble, might as well get started.

"Really?" Harold squinted at me. "Martha and I despise each other. I can't believe she'd even check up on me."

From what I'd seen of the receptionist, Martha despised most living creatures, and it also looked like I was already too free with my lies. Or at least not careful enough.

Barry saved me. "Everybody just wants you to feel better, Harold."

The old man actually smiled. "I do. This whole thing was nearly the death of me. Now that they've caught the culprit, Carla's coffee shop can open again." He grimaced. "And even though that means she'll put me back to work, at least this will be over for her, and she can move on. She's been through enough."

Once more Barry glanced my way. This was the cue. Somehow, we'd gotten there quicker than either of us had expected. "Actually, Harold..." He licked his lips, took a deep breath, and let his nerves show. "I'm afraid we... that I have some bad news. Part of the reason we came out here so early. I thought you'd want to hear it from a friend."

Harold flinched, sat a little straighter, and his left eye twitched. "What? What's wrong with Carla?"

Barry just shook his head, unfolded his legs, and slid off the bed. He held out his hand to me. "May I borrow the tablet?"

At his nearness, Watson emerged from under my chair as I pulled Katie's tablet from my purse, and he took his place by Barry's feet.

After I unlocked it, Barry took the tablet and turned it to Harold. "Have you heard of that food blog, the Sybarite?" His voice shook, and once more I hurt for having asked him to do this.

"Of course I have. Carla's been desperate to get into that. Thought she was going to have a conniption when that other stupid..." Harold's voice trailed off as he glanced my way, and then he changed directions. "Carla talks about it all the time. Reads it like it was the Bible."

Barry handed him the tablet. "Unfortunately, she finally got in it. But it's not good."

Harold paled and seemed to search Barry's face but accepted the tablet, and after a second, began to read.

Instantly he began to mumble, and his eyes grew wide.

"No... no..." His hands trembled, and he growled in frustration, then placed it on his lap so he could continue to read. "This says... It says..." He sucked in a breath, and his voice dropped to a whisper. "Of all the parched and pedestrian pastries I've tasted, only the scones of Black Bear Roaster are so repugnant that they exterminate everyone who partakes." Harold's gaze flashed up, panic filling it as he looked between Barry and me, then returned to the review. "Not to seem callous, but this food blogger has determined that those poor souls who perished had it coming. A review from years before warned of the dangers of giving patronage to Carla Beaker's Black Bear Roaster. The public has had ample warning. Unfortunately, now there's unadulterated proof. Hopefully, the coffee shop can be put out of its misery so it can quit inflicting the same unto others."

Harold was shaking so hard, I wasn't certain if it was nerves or if he was entering another seizure.

"We'll sue her," Harold practically growled. "We'll sue that Maxine Maxwell woman for all she's worth. Then Carla can open a chain of coffee shops. This is slander. And libel." He turned to Barry. "Get Gerald Jackson in here. Right now. I'm serious. We're going to destroy her."

Barry knelt on one knee and placed his hand over Harold's. "I'm afraid that's not an option, friend." Though his voice still trembled, I was surprised. I'd been prepared to jump in and take this part as I doubted Barry would be able to follow through. Maybe having Watson pressed against his leg as he began to lie gave him a little courage. "It's only libel and slander if it's not true, Harold. The police released the Pacheco kid this morning and arrested Carla for the murders of Eustace and Sally."

Harold reeled back in his chair, the tablet slid from his lap and the glass shattered on impact with the floor. Watson jumped at the sound but didn't leave Barry's side.

No one bothered with it.

"No, that can't be." Harold shook his head violently. "Carla didn't do it. She didn't. They can't arrest her."

"They found proof. Bananas had been added to several jars of the apple butter. Bananas that Carla had bought."

Barry had fumbled that line. That logic wouldn't be enough to place blame on Carla. I nearly jumped in to offer another reason, but it wasn't needed.

"I did it. *I* put the bananas in the apple butter." Harold's voice still trembled, but this time with rage.

Barry flinched, and he pulled his hand away.

I could tell he'd reached his limit. Knew he hadn't really believed Harold would say those words.

But Branson had prepared me for it. Made sure I knew exactly what they would need.

"Harold, it makes sense that you would want to protect Carla. She's your granddaughter, you love her." I leaned forward, making my voice as compassionate as I could. "But I was there when Sally died. You weren't. I saw you, Jonathan, and Maverick leaving as I walked in. Even if you had put the bananas in the apple butter at some other time, Sally would've had her EpiPen with her. Someone in that coffee shop hid her purse."

"I did that, you stupid girl." At Harold's outburst, both Barry and Watson moved away from him. "I moved it before I left. The stupid woman has the same routine every time she comes in. Apple scone with apple butter, to go with her stupid Apple name. Piles all her crap on the counter as she orders then spreads it over the table she and that other teacher use. I moved it as she ordered her first hot tea."

I was prepared to ask about Mr. Beaker, but he didn't give me the chance.

"And Eustace. What a waste that was. I had to be so careful to only get the cyanide on his scone, and then he goes and chokes to death on his own." Harold's face was bone-white in his rage. "If only I could have trusted Sally to have been as accommodating."

"Why?" Barry's whisper was so quiet that it was barely audible. He wasn't acting, wasn't going by the script, the horror and shock on his face was genuine.

"You wouldn't understand." Some of Harold's fury dissipated, just a touch, as he looked at Barry.

"Murdering people you've known our entire lives? No, I don't understand." Barry stood and took another step back.

"I wouldn't expect you to. Maybe you weren't one of the ones that benefited from Dolana's loss, but you went on to live a life of ease. There's no way you could understand."

Barry looked over at me, part in wonder, part in heartbreak at the confirmation of what I'd told him I suspected Harold's motive was. Then he refocused on Harold. "Are you actually saying this is all because of that property? After all these years, that's what this is about?"

"Exactly. All these years. That's exactly it, Barry." Harold attempted to stand, his legs shook so badly that he fell back into his chair. Even so, his voice wasn't suffering from any of the weakness. "You and Dolana were equal partners with the rest, but did they think of either of you? Did they think of *her* when they sold it for millions? Each of them got to live in luxury. She and I had to scrape by for her entire life."

"Dolana and I made our choices." Barry sank back onto the bed, his shoulders slumping. "The others held on to it for decades. You can't tell me that Dolana had an ounce of resentment toward any of them."

"Of course she didn't. She wouldn't dream of it. Too kind, too good. And more deserving than any of them, I promise you that." Spittle flew from the corner of Harold's lips. "It just makes it all the worse."

"You're right about Dolana. She was one of the best people I've ever known. And she would be so ashamed of you, Harold." For the first time anger lit Barry's eyes. "How dare you do this in her name."

Harold flinched, opened his mouth as if he was getting ready to yell, then sank back in his chair.

Part of me wanted to let it go, we had enough. Barry had been through enough. But I couldn't. "You tried to kill Percival with the car, didn't you?"

Harold looked up at me. All his anger was gone, he just seemed shrunken and spent. He nodded.

"No." Again Barry's voice was a whisper, but this time the horror in his tone outweighed anything that had come before. "Percival was her friend. I don't understand killing anyone, but he was *your* friend, Harold. Eustace and Sally weren't. They were awful to you; they were awful to everyone. But Percival..."

Harold just nodded.

I hesitated for a second, wondering if I should keep pushing, if it would hurt Barry too much, then decided we needed all of it, every ounce. "You were having a seizure. A real one. We saw you."

Harold continued to nod, and I thought he

wasn't going to speak. But then he did. His voice as withered as his expression. "I talked myself out of killing Percival several times. But then I saw him. I'd just taken Carla's car to get some space, try to figure out what to do after Eustace's death. The things everyone was saying about Carla... And then I saw Percival there. I just..." His parched tongue darted out over his lips, and his gaze fell to the floor. "I just cranked the wheel and hit the gas. I guess that triggered a seizure. I don't know. I don't remember anything else until I woke up in the hospital."

"Harold... how could you?" Barry sound utterly defeated.

At his feet, Watson let out a whine, and Barry slid off the bed and wrapped Watson in his arms.

It was enough. More than enough.

"Branson?" I angled over toward the door. Branson stepped in from where he'd been waiting in the hallway. "Did you get all that?"

There was admiration in his eyes as he nodded at me, and then compassion as he stepped in farther and saw Barry on the floor with Watson. "Yeah, Fred. I got all that."

NINETEEN

The following morning brought the largest crowd to the bakery portion of the Cozy Corgi that Katie and I had ever seen. Within an hour, every single pastry and loaf of bread was gone. We even ran out of coffee and tea. I hadn't realized that was even a possibility.

Even so, people stayed, filling up the bakery to the point I was certain we were violating a whole host of fire codes. But seeing as Shelley Patel, the fire chief, was gossiping with Susan Green over by the stairway, I figured we were in good shape. I also figured the world was about to end as Susan Green was darkening the door of the Cozy Corgi with some other purpose than giving me a hard time. If anything, she was the most popular one there. It was her day off, and people were using her as the official source of news. To my surprise, she seemed to be enjoying the attention.

Katie had started to launch into a renewed baking frenzy, but I talked her out of it. Instead, she sat at one of the tables by the windows with Athena, Paulie, Leo, and me.

"You know, I'm a little offended." Paulie, like the rest of us, watched the scene unfolding below our table. Athena had placed her purse on the floor, allowing Watson and teacup-sized Pearl to get better acquainted. Watching my grumpy little man cautiously sniff the bouncing white fluffball might've been the cutest thing of all time. "Watson always acts like he hates Flotsam and Jetsam. I just thought he wasn't a dog kind of dog."

As if to rub it in, Watson licked Pearl's muzzle in affection.

"Paulie, you know I love you, but get real, honey." Even though Athena addressed Paulie, she kept her attention focused on Watson and Pearl. I was certain she was worried Watson might change his mind. Pearl was smaller than some of the dog treats Watson devoured. "You know I love those two fury demons of yours, but they're crazy."

Paulie grimaced. "Yeah, I know. But still, I wish they could have some friends."

From what I'd seen from Flotsam and Jetsam,

they weren't sulking at their lot in life. I imagined Paulie was projecting his own desires onto his two corgis.

"They've got each other. They're good to go." Proving that Leo was as astute on humans as he was the wildlife in the national park, he pounded Paulie's back in that ancient form of male camaraderie. "By the way, I've been meaning to ask you. I've got some kid camp activities coming up this summer. Wondered if you'd like to help me lead some bird watching expeditions."

Paulie turned to him in slow motion, looking like he'd just won the lotto. "Me?"

Leo nodded. "Only if it's not an inconvenience. I know with tourist season—"

"I'd love to!" Paulie positively beamed.

Athena smiled softly at the pair of them and then winked at Katie and me before glancing down at Pearl, who appeared fascinated by Watson's knob of a tail. And for once, Watson didn't seem to mind at all. Satisfied, Athena refocused on me. "You had a good plan, Fred. And selfishly, I have to thank you. Writing that blog was one of the most therapeutic things I've done in years. Pity I had to set the status to private and only give the link to you. I'd love to actually hit Publish on that thing."

"I'm sure you would, but then you really could get sued." I didn't even try to suppress a chuckle. "Though, it would be fun."

"It was a brilliantly written post." Katie's tone bordered on reverent and was much more subdued than her usual. She'd nearly lost her mind when I told her the true identity of Maxine Maxwell. And though she tried to keep it covert, she continuously cast worship-filled glances at Athena.

"No, it wasn't." Athena let out a dark chuckle. "I allowed myself a little too much liberty, knowing it wouldn't actually be for public consumption. If it got out, I'd be more ashamed of the writing quality than worried over the risk of litigation." She gave a self-satisfied shrug. "But it did the job."

"It sure did." I reached over and patted Katie's hand. "So much so, that I'm afraid I now owe Katie a new tablet."

She turned to me, hero worship forgotten. "Glad you brought that up. I was looking at different possibilities online last night. It was about time for my old one to retire anyway. I'm considering some upgrades."

"Oh really?" I gestured around the bakery. "I'm thinking you can pay for those upgrades yourself, just based on today's sales alone."

"You really do need to get a helper in here, Katie. And quick." Leo leaned over the table. "From what I hear, Carla's is closed indefinitely."

Athena twisted toward him, resembling an owl as she craned her neck. Somehow, she even made that look graceful. "Are you serious? How have I missed that gossip?"

I *had* heard that gossip. I felt awful for her. "I hope Carla changes her mind. She's been through enough. All the drama at her coffee shop, finding out the things her grandfather did. That wasn't her fault."

The table was silent for a few moments. I could tell from Athena's expression that she didn't agree. Finally, Paulie looked my way. "That's one of the things I admire about you, Fred. Your sense of fairness and kindness. Carla's never been nice to you, yet, here you are, worried about her."

Carla hadn't ever been my favorite person in the world either, but my view of her had changed after learning how the town had viewed her family—how she'd struggled and fought to open her coffee shop only to receive constant criticism and verbal abuse from her father-in-law. Not to mention a certain owner of the Cozy Corgi having her best friend open a bakery less than a block away. "I think Carla has her reasons for being the way she is. Fairly decent ones, actually. I hope she doesn't give up on her dreams."

"Me neither." Katie scrunched up her nose and proved to be on a similar wavelength. "Somehow I wasn't seeing the bakery as competition for her. None of what she serves was baked fresh anyway, and I have much more limited coffee options."

"Goodness! You bleeding hearts are enough to drive a woman to drink!" Athena shook her finger at us. "Now, none of that. Carla is not innocent in all of this, never has been. Though I agree, she isn't guilty of murder, but it won't hurt her to do a little soul-searching. Now, I did come across some gossip..." She lowered her finger and an evil gleam entered her eyes as she focused on me. "Rumor is that a dashing police sergeant has reservations at Pasta Thyme this evening—a place that has quite the glowing review on the Sybarite blog, by the way, despite their small portions and exorbitant prices. Are we to assume that our heroine sleuth will be enjoying some housemade tagliatelle?"

I felt my cheeks burn, and I cast a quick glance toward Leo, who was fixated on something on the tabletop. I looked back at Athena before she could notice. At least that was the lie I was going to tell myself. "How in the world do you know that?"

"I'll take that as a yes." She smiled smugly. "And I have my sources. I like to stay informed about both my favorite restaurants and my favorite people."

Despite myself, I was pleased with the compliment. There was something about Athena Rose that made a person desire her approval.

Katie swatted at me. "You didn't tell me that!"

"We just settled on a time yesterday."

"When?" Her eyes narrowed. "As Branson was reading Harold his Miranda rights?"

I could feel my blush deepening. "Shortly after that..."

Before Katie could respond, Athena glanced under the table and sucked in a breath, then sat up straighter and looked around. "They're gone. They're gone."

"Who?" Realizing the answer before the word even left my lips, I glanced under the table as well. Watson and Pearl were nowhere to be seen.

Athena stood, scanning the bakery in a panic. "There're too many people here. She could be stepped on, and no one would notice until it was too late."

"I'm sure she'll be fine, Athena. We'll find her." Leo stood, followed by Paulie.

The five of us spread out, making short work of the bakery, then met at the top of the steps. "I'm so sorry, Athena. Watson doesn't normally wander off." Even as I said it, I realized that wasn't true. He just normally didn't have another dog with him.

Athena didn't respond but started down the steps, her lips thinned and her eyes narrowed in stress. It was the first time I'd seen the unflappable woman flustered. I couldn't blame her. She clearly felt as strongly about Pearl as I did for Watson.

The moment we entered the bookstore, Athena headed toward the front door, clearly fearing the dogs had somehow gotten outside.

That didn't concern me. Watson might wander, but he would never run away. I glanced toward his typical napping spot in the sun by the front windows, but he wasn't there. More out of habit than anything, I looked at my favorite spot in the bookstore, in the mystery room, and then called out to the others over my shoulder, "They're fine. They're in here."

The other four joined me in the doorway of the mystery room, and Athena started to rush toward Pearl, then paused at the sight. Her hand rose to her chest as she sighed. "Well, that's just the sweetest thing."

Pearl was asleep under the antique divan in front of the fire. She was perfectly safe and content with Watson curled protectively around her.

He woke at our attention and blinked up at me, though we didn't move. And I could swear I saw the battle rage behind his eyes. He had a reputation as the grumpy mascot of the Cozy Corgi, after all. One that he took very seriously.

Pearl snuffled in her sleep and nuzzled deeper into Watson's fur.

With a huff, Watson cast a final glare, tucked his muzzle around her, and gave up any pretense.

Katie and I had just locked up and were finishing a couple end-of-day chores when there was a knock at the door. This time, I instantly recognized the silhouettes on the other side of the door. It helped that there were two.

I raised my voice to be heard upstairs as I walked toward the door. "Katie! We have visitors."

By the time Nick and Ben Pacheco were inside the bookshop, Katie had joined us.

"You're Nick, scar on the eyebrow." I thought back to what Ben told me and then pointed at each brother individually. "And you're Ben, with the scar on your lip, right?" I didn't have to wait for confirmation as Watson zoomed over and shoved against Ben's legs.

Ben knelt instantly and began to stroke Watson's sides. "You got it."

Actually, with the two of them side by side, I didn't think I required scars or Watson. I couldn't quite tell what it was, but there was a tangible difference between the twins. Or intangible, rather. Though timid, Ben had a strong, quiet core to him, whereas Nick felt breakable somehow.

"Nick, sweetie, how are you?" Katie wrapped the lanky boy into a hug.

The poor kid stiffened, then relaxed into it. "Okay. I guess." His words were little more than a mumble.

Still petting Watson, Ben looked up at me. "I owe you an apology. You're the reason Nick isn't in jail anymore."

"No, I'm not." I shook my head and felt more self-conscious than I had all day. "He's not in jail because he didn't do anything wrong."

Nick met my gaze, and I saw a little bit of his brother's strength in his eyes. "Sergeant Wexler told me what you did after he dropped the charges. Said that even before you figured out who killed Mr. Beaker and Ms. Apple, you were convinced it wasn't me." The smile he gave, however, was nervous. "I don't know why you felt that way, but thank you."

The gratitude in the twins' gazes was nearly more than I could take.

Katie sniffed beside me, apparently feeling the same way.

"We won't take your time. We just... are grateful." Ben stood, much to Watson's dismay, and began to turn back toward the door.

"We never settled on a start date for you to begin working here." If I hadn't already made up my mind, which I was fairly certain I had, this interaction was the nail in the coffin.

Ben looked at me like I'd lost my mind. "Are you serious? You'd still offer me the job? After how I spoke to you?"

I laughed. "How you spoke to me? Ben, you're talking to a woman who has a temper." I pointed out my auburn hair, always my excuse when I gave in to that weakness. "Your defense of your brother was nothing. The job is completely yours, if you still want it."

"Really?" A smile broke over his lips. "I do. Thank you."

"No need to thank me."

"And what about you, Nick?" Katie piped up, and I instantly knew where she was headed. Though I wasn't certain if she'd already been considering or if the thought just popped into her head. Either way, it instantly felt right to me.

Nick looked at Katie with what seemed like fear. "What about me?"

"Well..." Katie sounded a little nervous herself. "Black Bear Roaster is closed, we don't know for how long, so you're out of a job. And if I recall, you like to bake. You never got to do that with Carla. You could do it here. I'm a good teacher."

He turned those wide, haunted eyes on his twin, then back at Katie. "You'd let me work here? Even after I was arrested?"

All nervousness left her as Katie moved closer and once more gripped Nick's arm in a motherly way. "No, I *want* you to work here. I want someone by my side who is passionate about baking. And you were arrested for something you didn't do. That doesn't impact anything." She released him but didn't move away. "You can take your time to think about it, of course. There's no pressure. We can even—"

"I want to." The words burst forth from Nick so fast that he startled himself. He laughed self-consciously, glanced again at Ben and then back to Katie. His voice was soft once more. "I want to."

The twins didn't stay much longer. Plans were made for them to start the following week, and Katie assured Nick that she would work around his schedule of classes the following semester.

And just like that, I had an assistant. I'd left the bookstore unattended so many times as I... snooped around, as so many people liked to say, that finally hiring someone felt like a long time coming.

"I know we hadn't talked about it, but somehow, the idea of them working here almost feels relaxing, doesn't it?" Katie smiled over at me as she locked the door behind the twins.

"Yeah. It does." Watson pulled my attention away for a moment as he trotted beside the window until Ben was out of sight. "Although, I'm not sure how much work Ben will be able to get done with Watson underfoot. I wish I could figure out what it is about a person that makes Watson go gaga. First Barry, then Leo, and now Ben."

Katie watched Watson as well and simply

shrugged. "I'd say it's a good sign. I'll try not to be insulted that he doesn't do it to me."

I snorted out a laugh. "Yeah, you and me both."

"Oh no. I just realized." Katie was halfway back across the bookshop when she paused and turned slowly back to face me.

"What?" From the tone of her voice, I was expecting something horrible.

She didn't answer for a second, just looked from one side of the Cozy Corgi to the other and then back at me, slightly slack-jawed. "With Ben and Nick working here, we're going to be three shops in a row each housing a set of twins. Verona and Zelda on our left, Noah and Jonah on our right, and Nick and Ben in the middle." She shook her head. "We're going to be known as, like, twin row or something."

She was right. "We can make it even better. You can dye your hair and we can be twins as well."

"Oh, sure." Katie scoffed. "Let me get right on growing half a foot so we can pull that off."

"No. Never mind. I like having you be short."

She glared playfully. "It's either vertically challenged or fun-sized, remember?" Katie grew more serious. "That is a high concentration of twins."

Another possibility hit me, and I slapped my thigh as I turned, calling Watson over from the window. "I've a better idea. One that allows you to keep your hair color and your stature." Watson waddled over to me. "How about we get a second corgi? *Watson* could be the twin." I ruffled his ears. "Would you like that, buddy? There could be two of you."

"Are you insane?" Katie looked at me as if I really was. "You do know that if you tried to bring in another corgi that Watson would kill you, right? Literally. Probably both of us."

I met Watson's gaze as I stroked him. "You wouldn't do that to Mama, would you?"

Watson cocked his head in a way that suggested he might understand me, and when his eyes narrowed slightly, the suspicion was confirmed.

Katie noticed as well. "See? Right there. He's plotting your death even as you speak."

She was right, of course, but I couldn't help but tease my little man. "No, you're not, are you? You want to share your treats with a little brother or sister, don't you?"

All concern left his eyes at that word. He let out a yip and began his bunny hop.

Katie chuckled. "I'll go get you your treat, Watson. I think you deserve one of the big all-natural dog bones you love so much for putting up with your mom's teasing."

Watson scurried after her, leaving me behind. But when he reached the base of the stairs, right before he darted up, he glanced back, with a very clear *Don't you even think about it, crazy lady* in his eyes.

TWISTER SISTERS MYSTERIES

COMING EARLY 2022

I can't begin to tell you how excited I am to finally bring this series to life. It's been in the planning and dreaming stages for over three years. The process was interrupted by my cancer diagnosis and all that came with it. A blessing in disguise, as the characters have kept me company over these years and have grown richer, deeper, and are producing a limited series (10 books in total) that is so much better than if things had gone according to *my* plan.

The Twister Sisters takes place in the charming Ozark town of Willow Lane. You've actually already met our three lead characters in the knitting group that crashed Percival and Gary's anniversary at Baldpate Inn in *Killer Keys* (the book where Fred and Leo shared their first kiss)!

You'll follow along with Cordelia, Wanda, and Pamela as they deliver their casseroles (Meals-on-Wheels style) and just happen to... you guessed it... solve murders!

The first three books are already up for pre-order, so you don't have to worry about missing their arrival!

And... this doesn't mean the end for the Cozy Corgi. Trust me, Fred—and even Watson—are cheering on their friends in their new adventure.

While Twister Sisters is a limited series, the Cozy Corgi is not. There's plenty of shenanigans ahead for our Scooby Gang.

Twister Sisters Mysteries

Katie's Scone recipe provided by:

2716 Welton St Denver, CO 80205

(720) 708-3026

Click the links for more Rolling Pin deliciousness:

RollingPinBakeshop.com

Rolling Pin Facebook Page

SCONE RECIPE

Ingredients:

    4 1/4C flour, all purpose

    1/2t salt

    1 3/4t baking powder

    1 1/2t baking soda

    1/3C sugar

    1C butter, unsalted, room temp

    1C buttermilk

Directions:

    1. Combine flour, salt, baking powder and baking soda in bowl and set aside.

    2. In mixing bowl with paddle attachment, cream butter and sugar until light and fluffy

3. Add dry ingredients and buttermilk 1/3 at a time alternating between the two until combined

4. Add desired flavorings such as extracts, nuts, dried fruits or chocolate chips.

5. On cookie sheet lined with parchment paper, form into round shape about 8" across. Flatten to about 1" thick. Cut into pie shape wedges into desired sizes.

6. Separate pieces from each other and bake for 15-20 minutes at 350 degrees.

PATREON

Mildred Abbott's Patreon Page

Mildred Abbott is now on Patreon! By becoming a member, you gain access to exclusive Cozy Corgi merchandise, get a look behind the scenes of book creation, and receive real-life writing updates, plans, and puppy photos (becuase, of course there will be puppy photos!). You can also gain access to ebooks and recipes before publication, read future works *literally* as they are being written chapter by chapter, and can even choose to become a character in one of the novels!

Wether you choose to be a villager, busybody, police officer, super sleuth, or the fuzzy four-legged star of the show himself, please come check the

Mildred Abbott Patreon community and discover what fun awaits.

Personal Note: Being an indie writer means that some months bills are paid without much stress, while other months threaten the ability to continue the dream of writing. Becoming a member ensures that there will continue to be new Mildred Abbott books. Your support is unbelievably appreciated and invaluable.

*While there are many perks to becoming a patron, if you are a reader who can't afford to support (or simply don't feel led), rest assured you will *not* miss out on any writing. All books will continue to be published just as they always have been. None of the Mildred Abbott books will become exclusive to a select few. In fact, patrons help ensure that writing will continue to be published for everyone.

Mildred Abbott's Patreon Page

AUTHOR NOTE

Dear Reader:

Thank you so much for reading *Scornful Scones*. If you enjoyed Fred and Watson's adventure, I would greatly appreciate a review on Amazon and Goodreads. Please drop me a note on Facebook or on my website (MildredAbbott.com) whenever you like. I'd love to hear from you.

I also wanted to mention the elephant in the room... or the over-sugared corgi, as it were. Watson's personality is based around one of my own corgis, Alastair. He's the sweetest little guy in the world, and, like Watson, is a bit of a grump. Also, like Watson (and every other corgi to grace the world with their presence), he lives for food. In the Cozy

Corgi series, I'm giving Alastair the life of his dreams through Watson. Just like I don't spend my weekends solving murders, neither does he spend his days snacking on scones and unending dog treats. But in the books? Well, we both get to live out our fantasies. If you are a corgi parent, you already know your little angel shouldn't truly have free rein of the pastry case, but you can read them snippets of Watson's life for a pleasant bedtime fantasy.

And don't miss book six, *Chaotic Corgis*, coming June 2018. Keep turning for a sneak peek at the cover.

Much love, Mildred

PS: I'd also love it if you signed up for my newsletter. That way you'll never miss a new release. You won't hear from me more than once a month, nobody needs that many newsletters!

Newsletter link: Mildred Abbott Newsletter Signup

ACKNOWLEDGMENTS

A special thanks to Agatha Frost, who gave her blessing and her wisdom. If you haven't already, you simply MUST read Agatha's Peridale Cafe Cozy Mystery series. They are absolute perfection.

The biggest and most heartfelt gratitude to Katie Pizzolato, for her belief in my writing career and being the inspiration for the character of the same name in this series. Thanks to you, Katie, our beloved baker, has completely stolen both mine and Fred's heart!

Desi, I couldn't imagine an adventure without you by my side. A.J. Corza, you have given me the corgi covers of my dreams. A huge, huge thank you to all of the lovely souls who proofread the ARC versions and helped me look somewhat literate (in completely random order): Ann Attwood, Melissa Brus, Cinnamon, Ron Perry, Rob Andresen-Tenace, Kelly Miller, TL Travis, Victoria Smiser, Lucy Campbell, Sue Paulsen, Chris Dancer, Kristine Zepf, Bernadette Ould, and Lisa Jackson. Thank you all, so very, very much!

A further and special thanks to some of my dear readers and friends who support my passion: Andrea Johnson, Fiona Wilson, Katie Pizzolato, Maggie Johnson, Marcia Gleason, Rob Andresen- Tenace, Robert Winter, Jason R., Victoria Smiser, Kristi Browning, and those of you who wanted to remain anonymous. You make a huge, huge difference in my life and in my ability to continue to write. I'm humbled and grateful beyond belief! So much love to you all!

ALSO BY MILDRED ABBOTT

Chattering Chipmunks

Vengeful Vellum

Wretched Wool

Jaded Jewels

Yowling Yetis

Lethal Lace

Book 24 (*untitled*) - Summer 2022

(Books 1-10 are also available in audiobook format, read to perfection by Angie Hickman.)

-the Twister Sisters Mystery Series-

Starting early 2022

Hippie Wagon Homicide

Casserole Casualty

Bandstand Bloodshed

-Cozy Corgi Merchandise-

now available at:

the Cozy Corgi store at Cafe Press

Made in the USA
Las Vegas, NV
04 September 2023